Dear Reader,

The Australian Outback [has]
a sense of loneliness and more than a hint of
danger. When my heroine Lily was stranded in the
Outback, and her only hope of rescue was
Daniel Renton—a scowling, unfriendly, reclusive
cattleman—she was justifiably scared. Her terror
might have shot off the scale if she'd known that
Daniel was only recently out of prison.

I love it when my muse throws up a situation like
that—a bubbly, warmhearted, innocent heroine and
a dark, powerful and dangerous man who has lost
his ability to love. In this story I loved the promise
of emotional risk and the knowledge that both
Daniel and Lily had a difficult journey ahead before
they reached a happy outcome.

Happy reading, and best wishes from Down Under!

Barbara

"I was selfish, Lily. I kissed you yesterday for all the wrong reasons.

"You drive me wild," he continued softly. "The way you fix your hair fascinates me. The warmth in your eyes touches me, deep inside. There's so much joy and beauty in you, Lily, and I—I wanted some of it for myself." His voice cracked and he had to take a deep breath. "I couldn't help it. I'm sorry."

"Daniel—" Her own throat was so tight her voice emerged as a croak. "For heaven's sake, don't be sorry." She swallowed and blinked. "I'm flattered—really flattered."

He turned to her. His face was in shadow, but she could see the glittering brightness in his eyes. She reached for his hands and felt them tremble at her touch. "And if you still feel that way, I'd really like you to kiss me again."

BARBARA HANNAY

Claiming the
Cattleman's Heart

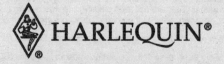

HARLEQUIN®

TORONTO • NEW YORK • LONDON
AMSTERDAM • PARIS • SYDNEY • HAMBURG
STOCKHOLM • ATHENS • TOKYO • MILAN • MADRID
PRAGUE • WARSAW • BUDAPEST • AUCKLAND

ISBN-13: 978-0-373-03925-8
ISBN-10:   0-373-03925-5

CLAIMING THE CATTLEMAN'S HEART

First North American Publication 2006.

Copyright © 2006 by Barbara Hannay.

This edition published by arrangement with Harlequin Books S.A.

www.eHarlequin.com

Printed in U.S.A.

Barbara Hannay was born in Sydney, educated in Brisbane and has spent most of her adult life living in tropical north Queensland, where she and her husband have raised four children. While she has enjoyed many happy times camping and canoeing in the bush, she also delights in an urban lifestyle—chamber music, contemporary dance, movies and dining out. An English teacher, she has always loved writing, and now, by having her stories published, she is living her most cherished fantasy. Visit Barbara at www.barbarahannay.com

Take another trip to the Outback in Barbara's next Harlequin Romance® book:
In the Heart of the Outback...
On sale April 2007

CHAPTER ONE

DANIEL RENTON dived into the cool, glassy water of the Star River. His naked body slid down, down through the dark green silence till he reached the feathery grasses on the sandy river-bottom. Then with a short, swift kick he arced up again and saw, high above, the cloudless blue of the sky and the tapering trail of smoky green gum leaves.

He broke the surface and struck out for the opposite bank, revelling in the cool, clean water rushing over his skin, between his bare thighs, between his fingers and toes, washing every inch of him. Cleansing.

Cleansing.

If only…

Daniel swam powerfully, almost savagely, as he had every day since he'd returned a fortnight ago to Ironbark, his Outback Queensland cattle property. But he always demanded more from the sleepy river than it could possibly give him.

Oh, the water rid him of the sweat and the dust and grime he'd acquired during a hot morning's work repairing fences, but it couldn't rid him of the rottenness that lived inside him. He doubted anything could free him from that.

He might be out of jail at last, but the emotional taint of his shameful months of captivity clung to him with a tenacity that no amount of bathing could banish.

Flipping onto his back, Daniel floated. The river was slow and he hardly drifted at all. It was always so wonderfully quiet here.

The birds had retreated into midday silence and the treetops stood perfectly still. The river was as peaceful and silent as an empty church, and Daniel tried to relax, deliberately blanking out the heartbreak and anger and pain that hunkered deep inside him. If only the darkness could float away.

He loosened the muscles in his shoulders, in his arms and legs. He closed his eyes.

'Hello! Excuse me!'

The voice, coming out of the silence, startled him. Splashing upright, Daniel trod water and looked back to the far bank. Against a backdrop of green and golden wattle, a figure in a floppy straw sunhat waved arms wildly, trying to catch his attention.

'I'm sorry to bother you,' a female voice called.

Daniel groaned. And glared at her. Who on earth could she be? Hardly anyone in the district knew he'd come home.

Still treading water, he shaded his eyes. The young woman was standing at the very edge of the water, leaning as far out as she dared and peering at him. Beneath her big floppy sunhat she wore a sleeveless white T-shirt that left her midriff bare and blue floral shorts and sandals. A woven straw bag hung from her shoulder.

A tourist. Not a local.

He didn't welcome any intrusion, but at least a stranger would be easier to deal with than someone who knew him. A local would be suspicious or curious, and Daniel wasn't ready to deal with either reaction.

'What are you doing on my property?' he growled.

'Car trouble, I'm afraid.'

Great. A city chick with car trouble. He released a deep, weary sigh.

A million years ago he might have considered a young woman with a broken-down vehicle a pleasant diversion. But his days of trying to impress women were long gone. These days he just wanted—no, he *needed*—to be left alone.

A year and a half on a prison farm tended to do that to a man. It robbed him of do-good urges. It had almost robbed Daniel of the will to get out of bed in the morning. What was the point in trying?

'I'm sorry, but can you help me?'

She was leaning so far out over the water she looked as if she was about to dive in and swim to him.

'Hang on!' It was a bark rather than a reply. This was a cattle property, not a bloody service station. But he struck out, swimming towards her in an easy freestyle. When he neared the shallows he stopped and stood in hip-deep water, his feet sinking into the weedy bottom.

The stranger on the riverbank was well disguised by her huge straw hat, but he caught a glimpse of light-coloured hair tied back or tucked up somehow. Apart from the snug fit of her blue floral shorts, she had a schoolmarmish air about her. Serious and anxious.

And yet… He could feel her studying him with frank interest. Her mouth flowered into an open pink O as she took in details of his bare torso.

'What's the problem?' he asked.

She gulped, and said a little breathlessly, 'I—I'm afraid I've r-run out of fuel.'

Immediately a bright blush flooded her neck and cheeks.

'I know it was stupid of me, and I'm so sorry to trouble you, but I don't know what to do.' Her hands flapped in a gesture of helplessness. 'I tried to ring the only person I know around here, but there doesn't seem to be anyone home, even though they were expecting me. I managed to coast down the side of the mountain, but then my car conked out at the bottom. I saw your gate and your mail box and so I turned in here, and your ute was on the track back there, and I—'

'Whoa,' cried Daniel. 'I get the picture. You want enough fuel to get you into town.'

Her face broke into an amazing smile. 'Yes.' She beamed at him as if he'd offered to fly her straight to Sydney in a Lear jet. 'If you could spare some fuel that would be wonderful.' Her warm smile lingered as she stood there. 'You're—you're—very—kind.'

Kind? A jaded half-laugh broke from him. It had been too long since anyone had called Daniel Renton kind—especially a young woman—and it had been even longer since a woman had stared at him with such obvious interest.

She continued to stand there, looking at him.

'We'll both be embarrassed if you don't turn your back while I get out of the water,' he said dryly.

'Turn my back? Oh. *Oh…* You're naked. Sorry.'

However, she didn't sound especially sorry, and she took her time turning, holding the brim of her hat close to her head with both hands.

'You're safe enough now,' she called, and her voice was warm with the hint of yet another smile. 'My hat makes great blinkers, and I promise I won't look till you say so.'

Mildly surprised that she'd stood her ground rather than make a nervous dash for the nearest patch of thick scrub, Daniel left the water quickly and hauled on his jeans without any attempt to dry himself.

'All clear,' he said gruffly.

She let go of the hat-brim and turned back to him, pink and smiling again—or perhaps still pink and smiling—and she watched with continued interest as he shook his head from side to side and flicked water droplets from his thick dark hair.

'I'm sorry. I'm being a nuisance.'

He shrugged. 'I was just taking a break. But I don't have a lot of time.'

Reaching down for his blue cotton shirt, he retrieved his watch from the front pocket and checked the time before slipping the watch onto his wrist. It was lunchtime and his stomach was rumbling.

'Where's your car?'

'Out on the road.'

'Not in the middle of the road?'

'No. I'm silly, but not totally brainless. I managed to push it well off the road. It's under a tree. I guess it's about five-hundred metres from your front gate.'

'What sort of vehicle?'

'A Corolla.'

'So you need petrol?' He bit off a curse.

'Well…yes. I told you I've run out.'

Daniel grimaced.

'Is that a problem?'

'I only use diesel.'

'Oh.' Two neat white teeth worried her lower lip.

'I guess I'll have to give you a lift into Gidgee Springs.' He knew he should have said this more graciously, but a trip into the nearest township would mean exposing himself to the questioning glances of prying locals.

'I don't want to put you to that much bother,' she said, obviously sensing his reluctance. 'If you have a telephone book I could ring a service station in Gidgee Springs. They should be able to send a can of petrol out here.'

'On a Sunday? You've got to be joking.' Daniel let out a hoot of laughter. 'I'll give you a lift, but you'll have to wait. I'm going to grab a bite to eat first.'

'By all means. Yes, you must have your lunch.'

After pulling on elastic-sided riding boots and shrugging into his shirt, he began to make his way through the scrub to the track where he'd left the ute, doing up shirt buttons as he went. The woman, ducking branches heavy with golden wattle, hurried to keep up.

'By the way, my name's Lily,' she said to his back. 'Lily Halliday.'

'Daniel,' he offered grouchily over his shoulder.

'Daniel Renton?'

'Yes.' He stopped, suddenly wary, and sent her a swift, searching frown. 'How did you know my name?'

Her shoulders lifted in a shrug. 'It's painted on your letter-box. "D Renton. Ironbark Station".'

Of course.

He sighed as he continued walking. He might have been

released from prison, but he was still constantly on edge and alert. Always defensive. He'd forgotten how to relax, how to trust. Simple details of freedom could catch him out. His name painted on his letterbox. A trip into town for groceries. A stranger's friendly smile. He wondered if he would ever again accept such ordinary, everyday normality as his right.

They reached his rusty old ute, parked in the shade of an ancient camphor laurel tree. He stepped towards the passenger door, intending to open it for Lily, but she clearly didn't expect anything so gentlemanly from him, and rushed forward.

'No need to wait on me.' Without further ceremony, she yanked the door open and jumped into the passenger seat.

By the time Daniel ambled round to the driver's door, Lily had removed her hat. And, as he settled behind the wheel, she slipped off the blue elastic band that tied back her hair and shook it free.

Her hair was heavy and silky, the pale colour of new hemp rope. It tumbled in waves over her shoulders like rippling water, and with a complete lack of self-consciousness she began to sift strands of it through her fingers. Finally, she lifted the full weight of it from the back of her neck, exposing damp little curls stuck to her warm pink skin. Then she re-twisted her hair into a loose knot and slipped the band back into place.

During the entire process Daniel watched, transfixed.

Eventually, Lily glanced sideways and realised he was staring at her. Their gazes met. And froze. They both held their breaths. *Something* happened.

Something in Lily's misty blue-grey eyes reached deep into the darkness inside Daniel and tugged. He felt an almost shocking sense of connection. It was completely unexpected.

Damn.

Lily gulped.

Oh, man.

Oh…man… It was crazy, actually, the way she was reacting to Daniel Renton. She'd made quite a fool of herself on the riverbank by gaping at his bare shoulders and chest. Such a silly reaction from a girl who'd grown up in the Sugar Bay hippie community, where skinny-dipping was an almost everyday occurrence.

Then again, how could she not be impressed? The tapering line from Daniel's broad shoulders to his flat stomach and lean hips would have made Michelangelo's David look like a mere boy.

And now, within the confines of his truck's cabin, mere inches from his face—from his blue eyes, deep-set and wary beneath strong dark brows, his jaw made extra rugged by a day or two's growth of beard—she felt distinctly breathless. She'd never met a man who was quite so devastatingly, so uncompromisingly…

Male.

Daniel Renton was masculinity distilled. And, to be honest, he was just a little dangerous-looking. So tense and guarded. Suspicious, almost. Fine shivers scampered down Lily's spine. Why would he look at her that way—as if she was a threat to him, as if he had something to hide?

Good grief, was she crazy to be jumping into a vehicle with a stranger? She'd been so desperate to get fuel she'd grabbed the chance, but had she been a tad reckless? Perhaps she should leap out of this truck right now and take her chances back out on the road.

Or was she overreacting? Perhaps Daniel's wariness was the natural reserve of a man who lived in the remote Outback.

She wrapped her arms over her bare midriff, but it wasn't her exposed middle he was looking at. He seemed preoccupied with her face, but she couldn't think why. Hers was a very ordinary face—a little too round, inclined to freckle, with eyes a nondescript shade. Seconds earlier he'd been looking at her hair—almost as if he'd never seen long, wavy hair before. Again, there was nothing remarkable about her hair. A very ordinary colour. Sandy—neither blonde nor brown.

Daniel lifted his hand and Lily jumped. For one breathless moment she thought he was actually going to touch her hair, and she felt a flash of fear. And then she felt something else that startled her, deep in the pit of her stomach—a shiver of shameless interest. What would it be like to be touched by this man?

But then he seemed to come to his senses, and his hand slammed back onto the steering wheel.

Lily let out her breath, and the muscles in Daniel's throat moved as if he was having difficulty swallowing.

Frowning fiercely, he jerked his gaze to the front. He seemed suddenly unhappy, and Lily felt unhappy too. None of this would have happened if she'd stopped for petrol in that last little town she'd so gaily flashed through a couple of hours ago. At the time she'd been singing 'Hit the Road, Jack' at the top of her voice. Now she cringed to think she'd been so naive, so foolishly confident that there would be more little towns, more places to fill up with petrol long before she reached Gidgee Springs.

Her thoughts flew to Fern, her mother. *I'm sorry, Mum. I've stuffed up.*

She grimaced when she remembered the pain in Fern's eyes as she'd waved her off this morning, smiling bravely. She would do anything to keep her mother out of a wheelchair, which was why she was on this journey. Her plan was to meet Audrey Halliday, her father's widow—the woman Marcus Halliday had married after he'd abandoned Fern—and to shamelessly beg Audrey for money for the operation Fern needed.

But now Lily's mission of mercy was in jeopardy. Totally. Unless this strange and taciturn man was prepared to help her.

While she was lost in her anxious thoughts, Daniel started the ute suddenly, and it lurched down the rough bush track at such a reckless speed that Lily had no time to fasten her seatbelt.

Toppling sideways, she fell against his hard shoulder. She tried to support herself, and her hand landed on his thigh, her splayed fingers gripping the denim of his jeans.

Beneath the thin and faded fabric, still damp from his recent swim, iron-hard muscles bunched at her touch.

'Sorry,' she squeaked, snatching her hand away.

He growled something incomprehensible and Lily didn't respond. Her heart was pounding unmercifully and, with more dignity than was necessary, she eased herself back into her seat and pulled the seatbelt across her and into place. Daniel drove more slowly, keeping his eyes on the narrow track. And Lily decided she had no choice but to trust him.

Their journey was rough going. Long grass grew between the wheel ruts, scraping the underbelly of the ute, and she recognised overgrown weeds—lantana bushes and Chinee apple—running wild along the edges, almost taking over the track in places.

As Daniel swerved to dodge another huge clump of lantana, she said, 'This property is wonderfully wild.'

'It hasn't always been like this.' He muttered this defensively. 'I—I've been away.'

'Travelling?'

He shrugged and continued to stare straight ahead through the windscreen. 'Not really. Just—just working somewhere else.'

'So have I,' she said brightly. 'I've been working in Sri Lanka.'

He sent a quick sideways glance her way.

'It was an amazing experience,' she said. 'I loved it. I spent twelve months doing voluntary work in a village on the coast.'

She looked at him expectantly, waiting for him to comment, or to tell her what he'd been doing, but he kept staring morosely ahead.

'When I came back,' she went on, needing to fill the uncomfortable silence, 'I couldn't settle into my old life in Sydney. The party-party-party scene just didn't cut it for me any more, so I went back to Sugar Bay to stay with my mother.'

'Sugar Bay? That's where all the hippies squatted years ago, isn't it?'

'Yes,' she said, but she sensed an underlying cynicism in Daniel's question, so she didn't elaborate. She certainly didn't want to tell him what had happened when she'd gone home— her devastating discovery that her mother was almost completely crippled and in dire need of surgery.

Fern had kept silent for too long. She hadn't wanted to tell Lily how badly her condition had deteriorated, had worried that Lily would come hurrying back from Sri Lanka too soon. Dear, silly woman.

The worst of it was that Fern had no health insurance and no money for the necessary operation, and the public hospital waiting list was up to two years long. Lily, unfortunately, had no money either, because she'd poured almost all her savings into the Sri Lankan village.

Fern had no choice but to wait in the long queue for the public health system, but by then she would be bedridden. She needed the operation *now*, which was why Lily felt compelled to face up to the woman who'd inherited every cent of her father's considerable wealth.

Lily sighed again. She could never think of Marcus Halliday without feeling the sharp, painful stab of his personal rejection. She'd carried the scar since she was five years old. Too long.

Daniel drove on in silence, and Lily realised the track was curving back towards the mountain range, which meant he was taking her further and further away from the road and into the wilderness. She felt uneasy again. Where was he taking her? Where was his house?

She had no idea if he lived with a family or alone. Good grief. Her imagination kicked in, throwing up dreadful possibilities. How on earth could she escape if Daniel was dangerous? If only there had been someone at home when she'd tried to telephone Audrey. Where was Audrey? She should have been expecting her call.

On the edge of full fledged panic, Lily squeaked, 'How far are we going?'

'Almost there,' Daniel muttered, and the track forked suddenly. He took a turn to the right, the track broke out of the scrub and two long, sun-drenched paddocks stretched before them. At the far end of the paddocks, against a majestic backdrop of heavily forested green mountains, a white homestead with a faded red ripple-iron roof and deep verandas sprawled in the sunshine like a sleepy dog.

Lily was buoyed on a wave of instant relief.

Tall, ancient palm trees surrounded the homestead, making it look cool, despite the shimmering noonday heat. To the right of the house, tumbledown machinery sheds were shaded by an enormous spreading cassia tree covered in massive, romantic pink blossoms.

'Is that your house?'

He grunted yes.

'It's lovely.'

She meant it. Daniel's house might not be grand or manicured, but there was something very appealing about it. She loved the way its long red roof reached protectively over the deep, shady verandas, and the way the green mountains stood on guard behind it. The circle of palms and the lovely pink cassia tree added a touch of romance. Undeniable charm. It was a setting an artist might feel an urge to paint.

Again she thought of her father. Marcus Halliday had made his fame and fortune bringing scenes like this to life on canvas.

Her lips pulled into a wry smile. Was it because of Marcus or in spite of him that the sight of Daniel's home tugged at her heartstrings? Whatever the reason, she felt charmed by the house and surprised, after her many misgivings, that she felt instantly at home.

'You must have been very happy to come back from your travels to such a lovely place,' she said.

Dark colour stained Daniel's cheekbones, and he cleared his throat. 'The house might look good from a distance, but it's run-down like the rest of the property.'

'So you've been away for quite some time?'

He didn't reply. Obviously he had no intention of telling

her anything about himself, but she wished he would. She'd feel so much more at ease if he was more outgoing. But, then again, why should he bother? It wasn't as if they were starting a friendship. Soon he would be dropping her into Gidgee Springs and they would never see each other again.

'The herd's been away on agistment.'

She realised that Daniel's focus was somewhere else entirely. He was studying the cattle in the paddock to his right.

'I only got this lot back last week.' Slowing the ute, he steered with one hand and leaned an elbow out of the window. He frowned as he fixed his attention on one particular cow with a noticeably swollen abdomen and udder. She was standing apart from the herd and looked rather uncomfortable, with her back arched and her tail raised. He brought the ute to a standstill, and Lily looked at the animal with sudden fascination.

'I need to quickly check that heifer.'

'Is she pregnant?'

'She's in labour. I've been keeping an eye on her this morning.' His thoughtful frown deepened. 'Usually there's no need to intervene, but she's young and this is her first calf.'

Without another word, he shoved the door open and strode to the fence, pushed the top strand of the barbed wire down with one hand, and swung his long legs easily over it.

Watching him, Lily let a sigh of relief drift from her lips. Surely a man who cared about a cow in labour couldn't be dangerous? She decided she might be safe with him after all, and her mouth twitched into a smile. How nice it would be if Daniel was as trustworthy as he was hot-looking.

He returned quite quickly.

'I think she's OK,' he said as he restarted the motor. 'But it's a bit hard to tell—the early stages are dragging on a bit.'

The truck rattled along the last part of the track leading up to the house. As Daniel turned off the motor, he said, 'I'm afraid it'll have to be bread and cheese for lunch.'

'Oh, I don't expect you to feed me.'

He frowned. 'Why not? Have you already eaten?'

'No.'

He gave an impatient shake of his head. 'Then come on. I'm going to eat, and you may as well have something. It won't be anything flash, of course.'

'Thank you.' Lily offered Daniel her warmest smile. But perhaps it was a mistake, because he seemed to freeze, and he stared back at her with such a fierce look that she felt her smile fade.

Three or four seconds passed, and then he said less gruffly, 'I can't treat you like a trespasser.'

Without warning, he smiled.

And, oh, what a difference it made.

Lily wanted to stare and stare.

CHAPTER TWO

THEY crossed the stretch of grass to the house and Lily saw that Daniel was right. The homestead certainly showed signs of neglect.

The long front veranda was unswept and littered with leaves. Dirty pieces of straw and old, yellowed newspapers were piled in corners. The white weatherboard walls were coated with grimy cobwebs and the windows were smeared with dust. Dried mud nests made by hornets clustered around the dark green windowsills, and long strings of grey cobwebs hung from the deep eaves.

Daniel sent Lily a grimly cautious glance. 'I did warn you. This is no showplace up close.'

She waved away his apology. 'I've seen it all before.'

He almost smiled again as he pushed the screen door open. 'At least the kitchen's habitable.'

And indeed it was.

It was large and clean, old-fashioned and homely, with a scrubbed pine table dominating the centre of the room and a big, open-shelved pine dresser on the opposite wall, filled with happy-looking blue and yellow china.

Actually, it was almost too neat. Where, Lily wondered, was the usual kitchen clutter? The feeding bowls for pets? The ubiquitous calendar on the wall with significant dates circled or scrawled over? And where were the old notes or receipts stuck to the fridge by funky magnets?

Of course, if Daniel had been away for some time, he wouldn't have had the chance to acquire pets or to gather much clutter.

'Do you live alone?'

'Yes.'

Was it her imagination, or had she seen a flash of pain in his face?

He turned quickly to the sink, squirted some lemon detergent and washed his hands. Over his shoulder, he nodded to a door. 'Bathroom's through there if you'd like a wash.'

'Thanks.'

The bathroom was plain but clean—with fluffy lime-green towels and a cheery sunflower stuck in a green wine bottle and set on the windowsill. From her experience of bachelors, the flower was an unexpected touch. Lily stared at it, wondering…

As she stepped back into the hallway she noticed that the doors to all other rooms, except one—Daniel's bedroom, she guessed—were firmly shut. Thick trails of grey dust drifted from beneath the closed doors.

Obviously he'd fixed up just enough space for his immediate needs.

She couldn't help feeling curious about him, about where he had been and whether he had a family—a girlfriend— even a wife somewhere. Why had this house and his large property been allowed to get so run down while he was away?

Ironbark Station would be worth a stack of money if it was a fully functioning cattle station.

And, now that Daniel was back here, why didn't he have help to fix it up?

No doubt about it, he was a man of mystery. Under other circumstances she might have felt compelled to try to solve his mystery, but right now her focus was her mother's health, and she wouldn't allow herself to be deflected from that. Besides, if and when Daniel Renton wanted anyone's help, all he had to do was ask for it. And, when he did, Lily Halliday would be the last person he'd turn to.

Unfortunately.

Over lunch, conversation was limited to 'Pass the bread, please' and 'Do you have milk with your tea?'—and Lily grew uncomfortable again.

She had always prided herself on being open and friendly and easy to talk to, and she found Daniel's reluctance to open up disturbing. It seemed odd to her that he would go to the trouble of offering to help her, even share a meal with her, and yet remain so reserved and secretive.

Her harmless question about whether he lived alone seemed to have silenced him.

It was odd. It didn't feel right. People in the Outback were famous for going out of their way to be friendly, weren't they?

She started thinking again about all the closed doors only a few steps down the hallway. *What was hidden behind them?*

'How anxious are you to get to Gidgee Springs?'

Lily jumped and looked up at him, to see his attractive blue eyes on her.

'Sorry. I was daydreaming. What did you say?'

'I was wondering if you're in a hurry to get to Gidgee Springs.'

'Why—um—why do you ask?'

'I'm concerned about the young heifer,' he said. 'I'd like to hang around a bit longer. Just to make sure she's OK.'

Lily lifted her hands, palms open. 'Don't let me stand in the way of a safe delivery. I'm keen to get to Gidgee Springs, but as long as I can collect my car in daylight it should be fine.'

'I promise to get you to town well before dark.' He shoved his hands into the back pockets of his jeans, and almost smiled at her. 'Thanks for understanding.'

'That's OK. Thanks for your help.'

Jerking his head in the direction of the paddock, he said, 'I'll head off, then. You're welcome to stay here at the house.'

'No, thanks,' Lily said quickly. Somehow she didn't fancy being left alone with all those closed doors. 'I'll come with you. I've never seen a calf being born.'

'You might not enjoy it.'

'I'm not squeamish.'

He stared at her for a moment or two, and Lily could feel his blue eyes piercing her, taking her measure, trying to decide if she would be in the way. At last he said, 'Come on, then.'

As she followed him, she remembered the succession of pregnant women who'd visited her mother in their tiny cottage in Sugar Bay.

Lily had been a child at the time, but, as far back as she could remember, the women had come, all looking alike in floating tie-dyed cheesecloth maternity dresses. And they'd always sent for Fern's help when it was time for their babies to be born. Usually Lily had been taken to stay at a friend's house, but occasionally she'd been allowed to play in another room in the house where the births took place.

She had grown up assuming that all babies arrived surrounded by the smells of scented candles, incense, and soothing massage oils, and accompanied by the gentle sounds of warm baths running, soft flute music and quietly issued instructions about breathing.

Of course, she knew better now. But Fern had helped dozens of women to have beautiful home-birth experiences, and they'd always shown their gratitude by bringing gifts— fresh eggs, fruit, vegetables and herbs, homemade jams or soaps and woven shawls.

Now it was Fern who needed their help, but her friends were an itinerant lot, and nearly all of them had drifted away from Sugar Bay.

The heifer was lying down by the time they reached her. Daniel retrieved a length of binder twine from the back of the ute. Lily wondered what it was for, but she didn't ask.

At the fence, he paused and held down two rungs of barbed wire with his boot, then offered a hand to help her over. Her legs were only just long enough for her to clamber over the fence without scratching her bare thighs, and she wished she was wearing jeans.

It didn't help that Daniel seemed rather distracted by her shorts. She felt a little flustered as she landed on the other side, and she had to grip his hand tightly to keep her balance. And then her hat fell off.

With an easy swoop of one long arm, Daniel retrieved it,

and at first she thought he was going to pop it casually on her head. But she should have known there was nothing casual about Daniel Renton.

He hesitated, and then handed the hat to her rather formally. But his smile was so unexpectedly shy and enchanting that she wondered why there weren't a dozen or more females buzzing about his property, offering to clean his house and to clear his lantana, or to fix him something more substantial for lunch than bread and cheese.

However, his smile vanished just as quickly as it had come, and he turned his attention to the labouring heifer.

The poor thing's sides were inflated as if she was holding her breath, and two little black hooves protruded from her rear end.

Making soothing noises, Daniel examined her with gentle hands, murmuring something Lily couldn't quite catch, before he began to tie the twine around the protruding hooves.

'It's just as I thought,' he said. 'The calf's a bit big for her,'

Lily winced, thinking of the pain. 'Poor darling.'

'I think she'll be OK with a little help.'

To Lily's surprise, he planted his booted foot on the heifer's hindquarter, gained leverage, and then began to pull down on the twine, easing first one little hoof and then the other.

The air was very still and hot out in the middle of the paddock, and Lily was grateful for her shady hat. The rest of the cattle were some distance away, grazing quietly, and all Lily could hear was an occasional chomp as they chewed at tufts of grass. And then the heifer bellowed sharply.

Lily watched the muscles in Daniel's forearms stand out as he hauled on the rope. She found herself holding her breath as she watched him strain, until at last the calf's gangly legs emerged. And then its head.

The little wet calf had a dark-red face like its mother, but there was a white blaze on its forehead. It looked so sweet. And then it blinked. Goodness, it was still in the process of being born, and it had actually blinked its cute brown eyes. Unexpected emotion choked Lily.

'That's a good, brave girl.' Daniel's voice was deep and calm as he spoke to the heifer while he hauled again on the twine, and the calf's shoulders inched forward. After several more firm tugs, the shoulders were cleared.

Again Lily held her breath, but it was only seconds later that the rest of the calf's body slipped out, and an involuntary cheer burst from her. Daniel sent her a quick, relieved grin and she had to swipe at unexpected tears.

'Oh, wow. Well done,' she said between sniffles. She stared at the newborn form. It was lying very still. Actually, the calf's eyes were closed now, and its chest wasn't rising.

Oh, no. A few minutes ago it had blinked so sweetly. How awful if it hadn't made it after all.

'It's not breathing,' she whispered.

Without a word, Daniel knelt beside the inert body. He broke off a piece of dried grass and calmly tickled the calf's nose with it. Lily couldn't help thinking how nice his hands looked—workman's hands, strong and callused, yet long-fingered and gentle. Hands that fostered life.

The calf gave a little snort and then another. Finally it lifted its head, and Lily gave a cry of delight. The new mother struggled to her feet and began to lick her offspring.

Still kneeling, Daniel looked up at Lily, his face alight, and she could see how very happy he was—almost as if he wasn't used to having things go so well for him. A breeze played with his dark hair. Lily swiped at her eyes and laughed.

'That was wonderful.'

She watched the skin around his blue eyes crease as he smiled at her, and he was still smiling as he rose lightly to his feet. Lily smiled back at him, and they stood there. They went on smiling foolishly at each other for a long, breathless stretch of time.

Daniel's eyes actually shimmered, and Lily's heart began to jump. She felt a thrilling, silent connection hum between them. Warmth. A special kind of happiness. And something far deeper.

But then he said, 'We'd better get you on the road again.'

Welcome to Gidgee Springs.

One-hundred metres from the weathered sign, Daniel pulled to the side of the road and left the motor running. This was it. As far as he was prepared to go.

He didn't look at Lily, but he was aware of her surprise that he had not taken her right into town. He could sense it in the way she stiffened and turned to him.

'That's Gidgee Springs,' he said, nodding ahead towards the straggle of houses on the outskirts of the tiny Outback town.

'So I see,' she said, but she made no move to undo her seatbelt.

Daniel grimaced and drew a deep breath that emerged as a sigh. 'I'd rather drop you off here than right in the centre of town.'

She didn't answer, but when he glanced her way he could see her confusion.

'Believe me, it's better this way.'

She sat very still, staring at him, her lovely eyes puzzled. She opened her mouth to say something and then thought better of it.

Daniel swallowed, and ran a restless hand around the steering wheel.

Again Lily looked as if she was about to comment, but she paused, as if she was thinking carefully before she spoke. 'You don't want people to see me with you?'

Daniel covered his embarrassment with anger. 'Look—I've done what you asked. It's only a short walk to the garage and you can get your petrol.'

His bad manners ate at him, but they were necessary. No way was he going to explain to Lily exactly why he was being so unfriendly. He knew it would make perfect sense to her if he drove her all the way to Jim Blaine's service station, waited while she got her petrol, and then drove her back out to her abandoned car. He had to go back that way anyway. He knew that. She knew that.

But what she didn't know, what she couldn't anticipate, was the way people would look at her if they saw her with him. He had no idea what had brought her to Gidgee Springs, but he was damned sure that her time there would be much more pleasant if she arrived without him.

'Jim will help you find someone who'll give you lift back out to your car. There'll be plenty of people happy to help.'

'I'm sure there will,' she said in a low voice. 'There have to be *some* friendly people around here *somewhere*.'

He could see puzzled disappointment written all over her, even though she was trying to hide how she felt. Well, too bad. This wasn't the first time he'd disappointed a woman.

With a sharp little tilt of her chin, Lily unclipped her seatbelt and pushed the door open. Her hat and handbag were on her lap, and she slipped the straps of the bag over her shoulder and picked up the hat.

Then she took a deep breath and looked at him, her face fashioned into a tight, polite smile. 'Thank you for lunch and for the lift. It—it was nice to meet you.'

His answer was a brief, bleak nod.

Her eyes flashed with an unnerving brightness, and with another spiky lift of her chin she stepped out of the ute and closed the door behind her.

She stood next to the car, and he had a clearly framed view through the passenger window of her blue floral shorts, hugging her cute behind, and above them the neat, slender curve of lightly tanned skin at her waist.

Clenching his teeth, he revved the car to send a clear message that he wanted to be on his way. Lily took the hint. With sunglasses and floppy hat in place, and her shoulders defiantly squared, she marched away from him. Her sandals crunched the gravel at the edge of the road and a gust of wind forced her to hang onto her hat. But she didn't look back.

Good.

Daniel shoved the ute into gear and executed an abrupt U-turn, sending out a spurt of gravel in the process. He wouldn't allow himself a single glance in the rear-view mirror. Another glimpse of Lily and he might weaken and head straight back to her, spluttering apologies.

For all sorts of reasons he mustn't do that. He needed to put plenty of distance between himself and Lily Halliday.

* * *

To Lily's surprise, it was a friendly young police sergeant who volunteered to drive her back to her abandoned car.

'Who gave you a lift into town?' he asked as they sped back over the bitumen.

'Daniel Renton.'

As Lily said this she hoped he didn't hear the quiver in her voice—a legacy of her lingering confusion about the man in question.

The policeman's eyebrows shot high. 'Daniel? Really?'

Deep down, Lily had guessed that her answer would surprise him.

'I wish I'd seen him,' he said. 'I heard he was back. I would have liked to say hello.'

He seemed genuinely disappointed that he hadn't caught up with Daniel.

'He was in a terrible hurry to get away,' she said tightly.

The police sergeant nodded, but didn't comment, and for several minutes he drove on in silence. Lily felt absurdly annoyed. What was the mystery surrounding Daniel Renton? Why was it such a conversation-stopper?

She turned to stare out at the passing rush of dry paddocks and gum trees, and gnawed at her lip. Perhaps it was just as well they weren't going to talk about Daniel. She'd experienced a ridiculous cocktail of emotions in the short time she'd been with him—intrigue, fear, sympathy—and an impossible attraction.

Daniel Renton was dangerously distracting. She hadn't experienced such a compelling reaction to a man since Josh.

Josh. Oh, help. She was hit by an instant flash-flood of emotion, piercing, sweet and excruciating. Josh Bridges was the blond, suntanned, beach-boy hero of her youth. With him, she'd experienced youthful infatuation at its most poignant and painful.

She'd invested far too many years in Josh, too much tender love and too many fragile dreams. Then, just as her father had done when she was five, Josh had abandoned her.

These days she kept her heart safely under lock and key.

Besides, she couldn't afford to be distracted by men. Right now, her mother depended on her. She was on a mission. Just as soon as she got her car going and was back in Gidgee Springs, she would try Audrey Halliday's number again, and she wouldn't give up till she got through to her.

But the annoying thing was that, no matter how hard she tried to divert her thoughts, Lily still felt an overwhelming need to talk about Daniel—especially to someone who knew him.

'Daniel told me he's been away and that he's only come back recently,' she said. 'I don't know where he's been, but I'm sure of one thing—he wasn't having fun.'

'You're dead right about that.'

'I could sense this…' She paused, and the sergeant looked at her expectantly.

'Go on,' he said. 'What did you think of him?'

'It's hard to pin down,' she admitted. 'But he seemed vulnerable somehow. And I thought there seemed to be an—an awful sadness in him.'

Lily drew a sharp breath, stunned to hear what she'd said. But, yes. Sadness. That was what it was. She hadn't been able to identify the exact feeling while she'd been with Daniel, but now she knew what had bothered her about him. Sadness. Deep, dark sadness.

The policeman was watching her with a shrewd, searching look, and then, without warning, his eyes twinkled. 'So Daniel brought out your mothering instincts, did he?'

'No.'

A second later, she regretted her hasty reply. Her denial had been an automatic defence, because she hated to be teased. But it wasn't the truth. And, for some reason she couldn't quite name, she felt that Daniel deserved the truth.

'I take that back,' she said softly. 'I'm not sure that *mothering*'s the right word. But he did make me feel—he did awaken my—er—sympathy.'

He frowned then, and his jaw seemed to lock into a jutting grimace as he stared thoughtfully ahead through the windscreen. Lily wondered what she'd said to make him look so serious.

Eventually his face relaxed and he turned to her, and she had the distinct impression that he'd made some kind of decision.

'Daniel deserves some well-directed sympathy,' he said.

She remembered the way she'd behaved when Daniel had dropped her off on the outskirts of Gidgee Springs. He hadn't offered any real explanation as to why he couldn't accompany her any further, and she'd been short with him, almost rude, and now she felt guilty. She felt impossibly curious, too.

'Why?' she asked, suddenly impatient to get to the bottom of this. 'What happened to him?'

CHAPTER THREE

THE sunset that evening set the distant hills on fire.

Daniel watched the blaze of red and orange from his front steps, where he sat, beer in hand, trying to absorb some of the twilight's peacefulness. He watched a flock of white cockatoos set out across the darkening sky with slow, heavy flaps of their chunky wings. And as the shadows lengthened he saw kangaroos and pretty-faced wallabies emerge from the scrub to graze in the long home paddock.

And he tried to forget about Lily.

By now she should have collected her car, and she'd be safely installed in the Gidgee Springs pub. Tomorrow she'd probably be on her way. Out of the district.

Just as well. He had enough to deal with without being sidetracked by a passing female.

Of course he knew why he felt sidetracked by Lily, why he couldn't get her out of his head. She was the first woman he'd been alone with in a long time. A very long time.

That explained why he was obsessed by memories of her hands fixing her hair. It was the only reason he was still thinking about her blue floral shorts. And her bare legs. The soft, touchable skin at her waist. And her eyes—the muted blue-grey of the sky when it was reflected in the Star River.

He let out a long, frustrated sigh. The fact that his mind clung to these details was proof of nothing—except the sad truth that he was a thirst-crazed man, emerging at last from the desert, and Lily Halliday had been his tempting oasis. That and that alone was why her smile haunted him, and why he couldn't forget the way she'd looked at him with uncomplicated directness, making his heart leap.

But he was going to forget her. Now.

In prison he'd taught himself how to forget. It had been the only way to save himself from going mad. He'd learned to blank certain mind-crazing images from his thoughts.

And now he blanked out Lily.

He concentrated on the darkening sky. Night fell quickly in the tropics, and already there was only a thin river of ruddy gold clinging to the horizon. Above it the sky was deepening from light blue, through turquoise and purple, to navy. And in his head Daniel named each colour, and imagined each hue blanking out a little more of Lily.

The blue…got rid of her legs. Turquoise, and her shorts were gone. Yes, yes, they were gone, damn it. It was good to be free of them. No regrets.

Purple—goodbye, midriff. Navy blanketed her eyes.

Almost.

He concentrated harder on the navy, willing the sweet, questioning look in Lily's eyes to disappear. At last. Mission accomplished.

Black took care of her hair…

And she was…gone.

He took a good long breath of warm summer's-night air and let it out slowly, savouring the relief of seeing nothing but sky. The stars had already popped brightly into place, and a thin crescent of new moon was peeking through the silhouetted branches of a huge gum tree.

The sky was huge and clear—and so was the land. It was good to be surrounded by all this space, by the country he loved. Ironbark. His country. If he worked hard enough, if he exhausted himself day after day, perhaps in time he would find his way back to the peace he craved.

He lifted the beer to his lips, realised it was finished, and considered fetching another from the fridge. But before he moved his attention was caught by lights bobbing through the darkness. Car headlights coming his way.

Cursing harshly, he leapt to his feet. He didn't want a visitor, but it was too late to turn out his house lights and try to pretend that he wasn't home. The car was moving quickly, its lights dipping and reappearing as the rough track wound through the scrub. His hand gripped a veranda post as he watched its approach.

There was a good chance, of course, that the caller was a friend. Daniel still had quite a few friends in the district, and they'd kept in touch. He supposed he wouldn't really mind if one or two of them wanted to visit. But he had enemies, too. And he was less certain of their identities.

The car was quite close now, and he could just make out its profile. Most people from around these parts drove trucks or four-wheel drives, but this was a small sedan.

Squinting against the glare of the headlights, he began to

descend the short flight of timber steps and wished he could see the driver.

And then, as the car zipped up the last of the track to the house, he recognised its make. A Corolla. A white Corolla.

A slim bare arm waved from the driver's window.

Daniel's heart began a drumroll.

'Hi, there,' Lily called to him as she jumped out of the car.

Her hair was no longer bunched in a knot, but hung loose to ripple about her shoulders in pale waves that took on the colour of moonlight. She'd changed into skin-tight blue jeans, and a black knit top with a scooped neckline. She looked fabulous—so fabulous Daniel felt his throat constrict and his mouth go dry.

Stunned, he stared at her. 'What are you doing here?'

'I've come to thank you for your help this afternoon.' She flipped him a dazzling grin, and then turned quickly to open the rear door of her car. 'And I've brought you some supplies.'

Too surprised to think about manners, he said, 'I don't need supplies. I've got what I want.'

'Daniel, you've got bread and cheese. And tea.' She walked towards him with her arms full of shopping bags.

'I like bread and cheese and tea. Besides, I've got beef. There's a piece of beef in the oven right now.'

She thrust a bottle of red wine into his hand. 'And here's something fruity and mellow to wash it down.'

Tightness in his chest made breathing difficult. What the hell did she think she was doing? 'This is crazy, Lily. You shouldn't be here.'

She dismissed his protest with another stunning smile, breezed past him and up the steps. From the veranda, she called, 'I told you. This is my way of saying thank you for rescuing me today.'

'But I don't need thanks. I don't want to be thanked.' With one leap, he was up the stairs and hurrying after her as she sailed into his kitchen and dumped grocery bags on the kitchen table.

'Don't look so scared, Daniel.'

Ignoring his protests, she carried a punnet of strawberries and a tub of rum-and-raisin ice-cream to his fridge. In two long strides he was across the kitchen, blocking her access.

'Just hold it right there,' he growled.

A soft gasp escaped her, and for the first time she faltered. She looked away, pressing her lips together. Then she took a quick breath, and when she looked at him again her expression was gentle and serious.

Daniel forgot to breathe. She was standing so close in front of him he could see the fine, clear perfection of her skin, the healthy and sensuous deep pink of her lips. The rosy scent of her perfume teased him.

'Don't panic, Daniel,' she said gently. 'I'm not here to stay. I don't want to invade your privacy.'

'Then you should go now.'

'Sure.' She sighed softly. 'Sergeant Drayton warned me you'd be difficult.'

'Heath?' He frowned at her. 'Heath Drayton? You've been talking to him?'

She nodded. 'He was the one who gave me a lift back to my car.'

His chest squeezed tighter. If Lily had been talking to Heath, there was a chance she'd been told everything—the whole sorry business. He felt himself gulping for air. This made less sense than ever. If Lily knew all about him, why was she here?

And then light dawned.

She was sorry for him.

She was overflowing with do-good urges, and she'd rushed back to Ironbark to bring him provisions in the same way she'd rushed off to Sri Lanka to help villages there. Daniel's shoulders sagged and he let his weight fall back against the refrigerator door. 'You want to turn me into a charity.'

She looked mortified, and turned bright red. 'No.'

'Admit it, Lily. That's why you're here, isn't it? It can't be anything else.' The last thing he needed was charity. From her. From anyone.

'No,' she said. 'It's just my way of saying thanks. I left you in a bit of a huff at Gidgee Springs.'

She sighed again, more loudly this time. 'Look, my hand is turning blue from holding this ice-cream. Can I get it into your freezer?'

His smileless gaze flicked to her hand. Her fingers were indeed mottled and purple. Without comment, he stepped to one side and Lily hastily opened the door to the freezer section, dumped the ice-cream and then deposited the strawberries in the refrigerator. As she slammed the door shut, she rubbed her cold hands on her jeans and her shimmering eyes confronted him again.

Her smile was tight, less certain. 'You can relax, Daniel. I'll get out of your hair now.'

Turning away from him, she gathered her dignity in the same way she had this afternoon when he'd dumped her on the side of the road, and she walked back across his kitchen with her head high.

In the doorway, she paused and looked back at him. 'There was just one thing I wanted to ask you.'

He swallowed, trying to loosen the lump in his throat. 'What's that?'

'There's a rest area about two kilometres back. Just off the main road. Is it safe to camp there?'

He'd been braced for questions about his time in prison, and was caught out by the unexpectedness of her query. 'Why would you want to camp there?' He frowned. 'It's only a picnic table and a rubbish bin. There's a pub in Gidgee Springs, you know.'

'The pub's completely booked out.' She pulled a face. 'I guess I should have checked before I came, but I couldn't imagine an Outback pub being full to capacity. I mean, Gidgee Springs isn't exactly a tourist attraction. But, just my luck, there's a big rodeo in town this weekend.'

'Yeah, of course. I'd forgotten. It's always on this time of year. People come from everywhere.'

'So I thought I'd try the rest area. I can sleep in my car. I'll be quite comfortable. It should be OK, shouldn't it?'

Daniel scratched nervously at the back his neck. A pretty young thing like her, alone in the scrub with no proper camping gear. It didn't seem right.

'It won't be the first time I've roughed it,' she said. 'When I first went to Sri Lanka our accommodation was very primitive.'

He shook his head. 'You shouldn't camp out in the bush on your own.'

'I wouldn't be completely on my own.' Daniel frowned, and she explained, 'I've got a dog.'

'A dog?' He stared at her blankly. 'Don't tell me you left a dog in your car all the time it was stuck out on the road?'

She rolled her eyes at him. 'Of course not. Heavens, Daniel, you're determined to have a poor opinion of me, aren't you?'

He shrugged. 'What else am I to think? You didn't have time to acquire a dog while you were in Gidgee Springs.'

Lily grinned at him. 'Of course I did. She's in the car now. Why don't you come and meet her?'

Without waiting for Daniel's response, she turned and headed back along the veranda and down the front steps to her car.

Scratching his head, Daniel cast a helpless glance at the grocery bags sitting on his kitchen table and then, reluctant but curious, followed her outside. At the bottom of the steps, he paused.

Lily had opened the rear door of her car and was bending inside, making coaxing noises. And then a skinny dog emerged. A kelpie cross, by the look of it.

'She's a stray,' Lily explained. 'She's been hanging about the pub for the last week, and the receptionist was in the process of calling the shire council to impound the poor darling. I acted on the spur of the moment and said I'd take her.'

The dog was looking up at Daniel with scared, almost pleading brown eyes. By contrast Lily, with her thumbs hooked through the belt-loops of her jeans, watched him from beneath lowered lashes.

'I have to admit, I thought she might suit you,' she admitted rather shyly.

'Me?'

He looked at the dog again, paying closer attention. Her thin sides were concave, and he could see that she was trembling. Her nose quivered nervously, and as she looked at him she made a soft, plaintive, pitiful sound, somewhere between a whine and a yap. Daniel felt his resistance crumble.

How had Lily guessed his fatal weakness?

How could she know that he'd be a total push-over, unable to resist this cowed and anxious, skinny mutt of a dog with huge, pathetic eyes?

'You were so good with the cow and her calf this afternoon,' she said, with a defensive shrug of one shoulder. 'And you don't have a dog. You're a cattleman. You should have a dog, shouldn't you?' Speaking quickly, like a telemarketer, she hurried to add, 'This one's very sweet, even though she's timid. But there's absolutely no pressure, Daniel. I thought you might like her, but if you don't want her I'll keep her. As I said, she can be my guard dog while I'm camping, and—'

Daniel held up a hand to silence her. 'You can't camp out there.'

'Oh?'

She looked suddenly worried, and he knew he had no choice. She'd brought him food to thank him for helping her, when in fact his assistance had been minimal and begrudging. She'd apologised for walking off in a huff, when she'd had every right to after he'd so ungallantly abandoned her on the edge of town. She'd brought him a dog, for heaven's sake.

How could he kick her off his property again and leave her to camp out on the edge of the road? If he was half-decent, he'd apologise for his behaviour.

'I can give you a bed here,' he said.

'Really?' Lily stood very still, looking at him with a wide-eyed yet careful expression.

Remembering that she'd been talking to Heath Drayton, he felt suddenly embarrassed and dropped his gaze. 'If you'll risk a camp-bed in my kitchen, that is.' And then, 'This is the only habitable space. The rest of the house is still a mess.'

He looked up, and she sent him a shy smile.

'Don't give the mess another thought. It's awfully kind of you to put me up. The kitchen would be perfectly fine. Thank you so much.'

Discomfited, he dropped to his haunches and fixed his focus on the dog. It bristled with tension, and he suspected it had been mistreated in the past. Holding his hand low, he patted the grass, but the dog stood her ground, trembling, watching him warily.

'Hey, girl, how're you doing?' He forced the gentle words past the continued tightness in his throat and clicked two fingers softly. 'Come on here. Come and say hello.'

The dog whined pitifully, and backed away two steps. But Daniel was prepared to be patient. He remained squatting, his hand outstretched but perfectly still, and he kept the soothing sweet-talk going until, eventually, the dog began to edge forward by cautious degrees.

'That's the girl,' he murmured gently. He glanced at Lily, who was watching him with a kind of heart-in the-mouth intensity, as if this were a life-and-death moment.

Slowly, the dog closed the gap and stood trembling before him, letting him pat her skinny back and then rub her head. Her tail wagged, and Daniel looked again at Lily, who hadn't left her post beside the car.

'Looks like you have a new friend,' she said. 'She likes you.' Her smile was tentative. 'I had a feeling you'd be a great dog-whisperer.'

'Thanks.' He said this sincerely. 'Thanks for bringing her. My old dog died while I was—away.'

He stood slowly. Across the metres that separated them, his and Lily's gazes met, and he felt again that involuntary connection, a tug of attraction, worse and deeper than before. He tried to think of something to say, but the right words evaded him. The dog pressed her nose against his leg, but Daniel couldn't drag his eyes from Lily.

Yellow light spilled from the veranda, across the tangled garden and over her, lending a pretty glow to her hair, her eyes and her lips. The deeply scooped neckline of her T-shirt accentuated her breasts. He almost had to close his eyes as an aching throb of longing took hold of him.

'Does she have a name?' he asked at last.

'At the pub they've been calling her Orphan.'

'Orphan? That's not much of a name.'

'She likes scrambled eggs.' Lily's expression was serious, but her eyes were bright now, almost smiling.

'Scrambled eggs?'

'Yes, she loves them.'

'Really?' His lips twitched and pulled up at the edges, trying to smile.

'I bought some eggs.' She nodded towards the kitchen. 'They're in one of those grocery bags.'

At last he smiled. 'You seem to have thought of everything.'

To Lily's disappointment, Daniel wasn't keen to investigate the groceries she'd bought, and they shared another simple meal—roast beef between slices of bread at the kitchen table. As they ate, Daniel's conversation was careful, skirting around any personal topics. In fact, they mostly talked about Orphan and other dogs they'd either owned or known. Beautiful dogs, ugly dogs, stupid, clever.

After their meal, Lily washed the dishes while Daniel unearthed a camp-bed from a storeroom at the back of one of the machinery sheds, and found bedding for her from a linen cupboard in the bathroom. Then, although it was still quite early, he said goodnight and retired to his bedroom. Orphan, who seemed hopelessly smitten by Daniel, followed him.

Left alone in the kitchen, Lily wondered if she'd ever get to sleep. The camp-bed was comfortable enough, but she felt too restless to settle. She could hear a bird calling mournfully outside, and every so often there were scratching and thumping noises on the roof which she guessed were made by possums.

But the strange sounds weren't the cause of her sleeplessness. Her mind was crowded with too many thoughts that chased each other like pieces of paper tossed about in a whirlwind.

She thought about the pain her poor mother endured—about Fern, waiting, patient and uncomplaining, as she hobbled about her little house at Sugar Bay. She sighed with frustration as she recalled the phone call she'd had when she'd finally got through to Audrey Halliday's housekeeper.

'Audrey's gone away. She's off on a shopping spree in Cairns, love.'

'But when I telephoned last week, you said she'd be home.'

'Yes, dear. I'm sorry, but Audrey can be so impulsive I have trouble keeping up with her. She'll be back on Friday.'

On Friday? Almost a week away!

It was so maddening. Lily hated the thought of going back

to Fern empty-handed. Fern wouldn't mind, of course. She didn't actually know Lily's real reason for heading off into the Outback. But that wasn't the point. Lily was convinced that she could solve her mother's problems by approaching Audrey, and she'd been so excited by the thought of her mother's surprise and delight when she returned with the money.

But how could she hang around in this district for almost a week?

Those thoughts alone could have kept her awake, but as the hands of the plate-shaped clock on the kitchen wall crept past midnight Lily thought most of all about what the policeman, Heath Drayton, had told her.

'You're bound to hear if you're staying in the district,' he'd said. 'Daniel Renton's recently been released from jail.'

Jail. Oh, God.

No wonder Daniel was withdrawn and shadowed by sadness.

However, when Lily had pressed the young policeman for details, he hadn't been prepared to tell her any more. 'But you can take it from me, they locked up the wrong bloke,' he'd said.

She'd been even more shocked to hear that.

Poor Daniel. How awful. The very thought of jail seemed to drain every ounce of happiness from her. It conjured dreadful images of dreary grey guarded cells, walls topped by broken glass and barbed wire, lines of angry men, degraded and defeated.

On the other hand, although it was a selfish thought, she was reassured to know that at least her instincts about Daniel had been right. He was a troubled man, but apparently he wasn't really a criminal.

'I'm afraid Daniel will still have a few dry gullies to cross, emotionally,' Heath had added, and his eyes had flashed with a disturbing shrewdness.

Lily had felt compelled to protest. 'I don't have designs on him.'

He'd grinned at her then. 'That's a damn shame.'

No wonder she couldn't sleep.

CHAPTER FOUR

WHEN Daniel looked in at the kitchen door next morning, Lily was still fast asleep. She was lying on her back, her tanned arm, loose with sleep, flung over the pillow. A single gold bangle encircled her wrist. She looked innocent and lethal at once—sweet, and yet dangerously sensuous and womanly.

He couldn't help staring at her—spellbound by the perfect swell of her breasts beneath a lavender camisole, by her softly parted lips, the pink flush on her cheeks, the play of morning sunlight spinning her sandy hair to silver and gold. He was seized by a desperate desire to plunge his hands in her hair. He wanted to touch her soft skin, to taste her lips and to kiss the shallow dip above her collarbone, to bury his face in her breasts.

He wanted her—wanted her so badly he almost groaned aloud with the aching thrust of his need.

Damn.

Spinning on his heel, he made a hasty but necessary exit. Breakfast could wait. He'd put in two full hours of work before he ventured back into his kitchen.

Five minutes later, steering the tractor towards a stand of head-high kunai grass, he went through the process of banishing all thoughts of Lily. But when at last he'd cleared his head of her he made a mistake. A bad mistake.

He thought about Jess instead.

Jessica, his daughter, who lived in Sydney with his former mother-in-law. Thinking of her brought the full weight of his awful loneliness down on him. The memories of Jess crowded in—especially the way she'd used to dance into the kitchen on weekday mornings, dressed in her blue-and-white-checked school uniform with her pigtails bobbing, eager to guess what he'd prepared for her breakfast.

Sometimes it had been sausages or baked beans, but more often than not it had been eggs—boiled, poached, scrambled or fried. Her favourite was a boiled egg in a hen-shaped egg-cup. And she'd have toast fingers for dipping. And milk, or orange juice, in a glass with stars painted on it.

In winter she'd have porridge, sprinkled with brown sugar. Saturday mornings they'd made pancakes sprinkled with white sugar and lemon juice.

Food was a big deal for Jess. She was always ravenous. And yet, because she was always on the go, she was such a skinny little thing. All thin brown limbs and big blue eyes. Full of laughter. Lots of laughter. And hugs. And giggles. Oh, boy, could that kid giggle.

Daniel pressed a fisted hand over his mouth to stop himself from crying out.

Life without Jess was hell.

He thought of the breakfast he'd had yesterday morning— dry toast and black tea. It was all he'd felt like.

He'd read somewhere that a lack of interest in food was a symptom of depression. Well, yeah, maybe he was depressed. Maybe he had a right to be down. Freedom wasn't all it was cracked up to be—not when it meant coming home to a run-down property with too many broken fences, overgrown weeds and heavily reduced numbers of stock in poor condition.

And an empty house.

Without Jess.

He had little hope of ever winning his daughter back from his former mother-in-law's clutches.

'You can't possibly expect Jess to live with you *now*, Daniel,' Susan had told him, her smug, well-bred voice turning shrill over a long-distance phone call from Sydney. 'Not after all that she's been through. Have you any idea how she's suffered during your—your *incarceration*? I won't countenance sending her back. It's unthinkable. She's only just settling down now, and it would be cruel to disturb her. Besides, you couldn't be an appropriate person to take care of a young girl turning eleven. She's at a very delicate age.'

Oh, yeah, Susan. And you did such a superb job of raising your own daughter.

When he ventured back to the house at around eight, he saw that Lily had folded the camp-bed and set it on the veranda, and as he approached the kitchen doorway he was met by the mouthwatering aroma of frying bacon. Lily was at his stove, frying not only bacon, but mushrooms, tomatoes and eggs.

She turned and grinned at him. 'I started as soon as I heard your tractor stop.'

His stomach rumbled as he eyed the sizzling pan. 'Did you buy all this stuff in town yesterday?'

'I sure did. There's orange juice in the fridge, and I've got some freshly ground coffee from New Guinea. Would you like some?'

He was suddenly incredibly hungry.

'Orange juice and coffee would be great,' he admitted, and he reached to open a cupboard. 'I'm sure there's a coffee plunger in here somewhere.'

As they sat down to breakfast, Lily wondered if this would be another meal accompanied by desultory, awkward conversation. If only Daniel was relaxed and sociable, like most of her friends, then he would probably ask her what her plans were. And she would feel quite free to tell him about her reason for being here, about her worries for Fern and her need to confront Audrey—as well as her frustration with the scarcity of accommodation at the pub, and how Audrey had taken off without notice.

And once she'd explained all that it would be more than likely that a relaxed and sociable friend would invite her to stay on. She would offer to clean his house in exchange for accommodation. Heaven knew, Daniel could do with a helping hand.

But Daniel was nowhere near relaxed—which was hardly surprising, given all that he'd been through.

Eighteen months in prison.

Lily couldn't imagine shaking off an experience like that. And Heath Drayton had implied that Daniel certainly should not have been locked up in the first place. If he was innocent—and Lily had no doubt that he was—he might never get over the cruel injustice of it. No wonder a pall of black gloom clung to the man. He couldn't be expected to forget such horror quickly or easily.

'So, you're heading off today?' His voice cut through her thoughts, catching her off-guard. 'Which way are you going? Back to Sugar Bay?'

What was the point of lying? She had nothing to lose by telling him the truth. 'Actually, I was hoping to see someone who lives out here. But she's gone away, so I'm at a bit of a loose end for a few days.'

He looked displeased with her answer, and frowned moodily as he speared a mushroom with his fork.

She felt a ridiculous urge to give him a bear hug and urge him to cheer up, but then she remembered about the 'emotional dry gullies' he still had to cross.

Ridiculous urge, indeed.

Instead, she said quickly, nervously, 'Look, Daniel, I'll keep out of your way, I promise, but I was wondering if perhaps I could give you a hand to clean this place up?'

He looked shocked. 'Why would you want to do that?'

Lily sucked in a quick breath. 'Well, for starters, the pub's full.' She began to tick off the points on her fingers. 'And you've got a problem with me camping down by the road. You've got more than enough on your plate with the cattle and weeds and things, so you don't have time for your house. I'm cash-strapped and need somewhere to stay.'

When he didn't respond, she went on. 'Maybe I could do a spot of house-cleaning?'

It was simply a practical arrangement that benefited them both, Lily told herself. But was she being honest? She hated to think about 'moth and flame' comparisons, but she'd felt shamelessly drawn to Daniel ever since she'd first seen him standing in the river, naked and wet, with muscles rippling.

And her feelings for him had become more complicated once she'd learned that he'd been in jail. When she looked at him now, she felt a sweet, piercing pang that went deep—way deeper than sympathy. Or simple lust.

So, yes, for all sorts of reasons she was probably crazy to be here, proposing to intrude further into this man's home.

But the alternative—heading home empty-handed—would feel like bitter defeat, as if her father had won after all.

Daniel stared at her, and his throat worked, and then he dropped his gaze to Orphan, who was sitting quietly near his feet. 'I don't have much in the way of cleaning gear,' he said.

Good heavens. Was she mistaken, or had that sounded amazingly like an acceptance?

Lily cleared her throat. 'I could run into Gidgee Springs and stock up for you, if you like.'

His head jerked up, and he eyed her warily. 'If people in town knew you were working for me they could give you a hard time.' A dark flush stained his cheekbones.

'I'd like to see them try.' Reaching a hand across the table, she almost, but not quite, touched him. 'Daniel, I don't know why you went to prison, but Heath Drayton told me they jailed the wrong man. That's good enough for me. I believe him. I don't care what others think or say.' She tried to make a joke of it. 'I was brought up in a hippie commune. I'm a free spirit.' She lifted an eyebrow. 'I also perform miracles with dusting rags.'

Daniel refused to be amused. Jaw set, he stared at Orphan, and seemed to be wrestling with an inner battle.

'I've got a vacuum cleaner,' he said at last. 'Not much else.'

Lily's breath caught. 'Great. A cobweb broom would be

handy, too. And I could get extra bottles of cleaning stuff. Furniture polish—that sort of thing. What do you reckon?'

She waited for his scowl, but, to her surprise, he smiled slowly.

'I reckon you've got a huge job on your hands.'

She smiled sweetly back at him. 'I like a challenge.'

I like a challenge?

Mid-morning, Lily stood in the hallway of Daniel's house, surrounded by a mountain of cleaning equipment, and wished she'd been more honest with him. With herself.

If she'd been truthful she would have admitted that her housekeeping skills were minimal. In fact, when she'd lived in Sydney she'd paid a weekly cleaning service to take care of her tiny, one-bedroom apartment. She'd had better things to do than mopping and dusting—she'd had parties to attend, nightclubs and the movies.

Travelling to Sri Lanka had changed her. Rather, it had completed a change that had already begun. For some time before that she'd been growing more and more uneasy with her shallow, frivolous lifestyle in Sydney. After twelve months of working in disaster-ravaged villages, she'd discovered the deeper satisfaction of helping people who desperately needed her help but could never pay her back in a material sense.

However, she'd been working in administration, writing begging letters for donations, placing orders for essential commodities and distributing provisions—not doing housework.

Now Lily's chest was spiked by an uncomfortable twinge of guilt. Not because she couldn't work out how to turn on the vacuum cleaner, but because by boasting about non-existent housekeeping skills she'd been given permission to invade Daniel's home. He clearly didn't want to talk about himself or his past, and yet she would be opening doors that would reveal all manner of things about him—and, possibly, about the people who had lived with him.

She hoped, as she set her hand on the first doorknob, that she wasn't making a serious mistake.

She felt nervous flutters in her stomach. For all she knew, there might be very good reasons why Daniel had left these doors shut. She'd assumed he simply wanted to contain the dust, but they could be hiding anything—including bad memories.

Nevertheless, she was committed now. He'd gone off with Orphan to mend fences and left her the run of his house.

Her original plan had been to throw open all the doors and get an overall idea of what she was up against. But now the thought of five filthy rooms was too daunting, and it suddenly seemed prudent to uncover the rooms one at a time—a kind of lucky dip.

She pushed the first door open.

It wasn't until she heard Daniel's footsteps coming down the hall that she realised it was lunch time already, and she was only halfway through cleaning the first room.

She was on her knees beside the bookcase, surrounded by small towers of books, busy with a bottle of orange oil and a dusting rag, but she sent Daniel a brave smile as he came into the room. And his answering smile was surprisingly warm. It seemed to slip right under her skin, warming every part of her.

Hoping to deflect attention from her slow progress, she asked quickly, 'How did Orphan enjoy her first morning at Ironbark?'

Daniel was so busy looking around him at the room that he almost seemed to have forgotten the dog at his heels. He blinked and looked down at Orphan. 'I think she's had a great time. She actually chased a wallaby. What about you?'

'I'm afraid I'm terribly slow at this.' She hoped he didn't see the guilty flash in her eyes. 'I expected to be finished with this room already, but I realised these books needed to be dusted individually.'

'Whatever you're doing, the results are great.' He continued to look about the large, airy room, with rows of deep, white-framed windows that opened onto the veranda. 'I'd forgotten how much I liked this living room.'

'I took the curtains down,' Lily said. 'But I'm afraid they might not survive another wash, or even a trip to the cleaners. They look as if they might fall to pieces.'

Daniel surveyed the framed-glass windows, now sparkling clean and offering a clear view of the front lawn, the pink cascading flowers of the cassia tree and the sunny blue sky above. 'I think I prefer it in here without curtains.'

Resting back on her heels, Lily considered this. 'I don't suppose privacy's an issue out here, but you might want some sort of drape to cut the afternoon sun if you're watching television.'

'Perhaps.' He frowned, and something like a shadow passed across his face. 'I haven't bothered with television since I got back. Somehow I haven't felt ready to let the outside world in.'

This unexpected admission brought a lump to Lily's throat. It was the first time Daniel had shown her a tiny glimpse into how he was feeling.

He crossed the room and ran his fingers lightly along the back of the sofa, and then he stared thoughtfully at the silky oak entertainment centre, housing a television set, a CD player and a video recorder. The freshly polished timber gleamed with a warm honey glow, and as he studied it he seemed lost in thought. In memories?

Lily wondered if he was remembering happy times, sitting there on the sofa with someone he loved curled beside him while they watched their favourite TV show, or perhaps a movie. She could picture a bowl of popcorn on the coffee table. Or wine glasses. Two heads close together.

A loud and very unhappy sigh escaped Daniel, making Lily uncomfortable, as if she were a voyeur, watching him during an intensely private moment. She discreetly switched her attention to Orphan, who was sniffing and snuffling at something in the corner behind a lounge chair.

'You're showing me up, Orphan,' she said, with a bright little laugh. 'I know I haven't cleaned in that corner yet. What have you found? A dead mouse?'

Hurrying over, she bent down to see what the dog was so interested in. 'Oh, dear, no, you can't have that.' Over her shoulder, she told Daniel. 'It's a poor little dried-out frog. It must have hopped in here and then couldn't find its way out again.'

'Don't let Orphan eat it,' he said. 'It might be a cane toad. They're poisonous.'

'It's all right. I've wrapped it up in a duster.'

Lily patted the dog's head, but in a distracted way. She'd seen something else down on the floor—a dusty cherrywood frame. Bending lower, she reached into the corner behind the chair. 'There's something wedged back here. It looks like a photo frame.'

Standing upright again, she held it out, and Daniel's face tightened.

'That's nothing,' he snapped. 'It can go straight in the bin.'

Lily knew she should probably do exactly as he asked, but she was seized by insatiable curiosity and she turned the frame over. She couldn't help a shocked gasp. Despite the dust and cobwebs that covered it, she could see that this was a wedding photo.

Daniel, as a young bridegroom, looked impossibly happy and proud beside his beautiful bride—a stunning, slender brunette in an exquisite Italian gown.

Heat tinged Lily's cheeks and her throat grew tight. Where was that bride now?

'Give it here,' Daniel muttered. 'I'll get rid of it.'

'All right.' She stepped forward and handed it to him. He took it from her a little too roughly. 'Be careful,' she warned. 'The glass is broken.'

He scowled at her, and then at the photo.

What should she say? What *could* she say? 'She's a very lovely bride.'

'She's dead.'

The two words struck her like knife-thrusts.

She's dead. Oh, my God.

Sickened, Lily saw that Daniel was holding the frame by one corner, between two fingers, as if it were a letter bomb. She saw again, beneath the fractured, dusty glass, the beautiful face of the young bride, and she was seized by the terrible thought that this woman's death was the reason Daniel had gone to jail.

She felt a flare of panic. Her horrified imagination raced, throwing up wild pictures of terrible possibilities—a domestic dispute that got out of hand, an unhappy love triangle, a passionate duel…

Shocked, shaken, she stared down at her hands. They were trembling. She knew her face must have drained of colour. 'I—I'm so sorry.'

'Don't be sorry for me.'

Lily flinched. 'I—I…' She wrung her hands wretchedly. Why, oh, why, had she dragged that photo out? She felt again all the old fears that had haunted her when she'd first met Daniel. Who was he? What had happened? What had she got herself into?

'I didn't know,' she said softly. 'I—I mean, I don't know anything—about—about you. I shouldn't have—'

She stopped, knowing that her stammering awkwardness was only making things worse.

Daniel stared at her, his face devoid of all warmth. He stood granite-still, and his eyes were dark grey stones. Lily felt so scared, she wished she could gather up her things and run away.

'You think I killed Cara?' he asked in a hoarse whisper.

Frightened by the cold light in his eyes, she shook her head. 'No. Not—' She had been going to say *not intentionally*, but the awful steel in his eyes stopped her.

After a dreadful silence, Daniel said, 'There's no connection between my wife's death and my jail sentence. Cara died six years ago. And she'd already left me a year before she died.'

'Oh, I—I see,' Lily whispered, and then she was swamped with relief. Daniel hadn't killed his wife. Almost immediately, she felt a rush of sympathy for him. The poor man! How many tragedies had shadowed his life?

He turned abruptly away and stared out of the window. 'This is exactly what I hoped to avoid,' he said harshly. 'A total stranger digging up all the unhappy details of my personal life.'

'I'm sorry,' she said in a small, tight voice. 'I didn't want to intrude into your personal matters. I know this must be painful for you. I wanted to help, but if my poking around brings back too many bad memories—'

A bitter, mocking laugh escaped him. 'Will you leave off the "poor, wounded Daniel" routine? I don't need your sympathy, Lily. Believe me. I can talk about my marriage without bursting into tears. I'm past all that. Our marriage was a mistake from the start.'

Turning from the window, he said, less severely, 'Cara ended up with a property developer from Sydney—a guy from the fast lane. Someone who could keep her in fancy clothes and fancy cocktails. And, more importantly, someone her mother approved of.'

Then he walked across the room and dropped the photo into the plastic garbage bag Lily had been using for rubbish. He wiped his hands against each other to rid them of dust, then plunged them into his jeans pockets and stood, staring at the floor.

'I should amend that. Cara's mother thought the new guy was wonderful,' he said. 'Until he ran his BMW over a cliff one morning on his way home from an all-night party. Taking her daughter with him.'

An uncomfortable silence descended.

Lily thought for a moment that now Daniel had started he might go on to tell her more—even about why he'd gone to jail. But after another uncomfortable stretch of silence she realised that wasn't going to happen. As he said, he hated the idea of a total stranger learning all the unhappy details of his personal life.

'Daniel,' she said, and then she had to stop to swallow the nervous knot in her throat. 'I truly wanted to help, but if my going through your house brings back things you'd rather forget, perhaps I'm really not much use to you.'

He was still standing by the rubbish bag with his hands deep in his pockets, his eyes less stony, but not exactly friendly.

Lily straightened her shoulders and drew a deep breath. This house was an emotional landmine. She should walk away now, before she stepped on something really disastrous.

'I'm afraid I've disturbed your peace,' she said.

He looked at her from across the room. 'You disturb my peace in more ways than you might guess, Lily. I might have a poor way of showing it, but I do appreciate your help.'

His blue eyes were suddenly alight with a warm, soft glow, and he actually smiled at her. Lily felt again an unexpected, inescapable pull, so strong she almost cried out.

'I appreciate your company, too,' Daniel said, and he smiled again.

Heaven help her. When he smiled at her that way, all thoughts of running away evaporated like mist at sunrise. Perhaps this moment—finding the photograph—was one of the 'dry gullies' Heath Drayton had referred to. And Daniel had crossed it. They both had—and they'd safely reached the other side.

'Well,' Lily said, with a renewed lightness of heart. 'I guess it's time to get lunch ready. I'm starving, aren't you?'

The fencing Daniel had scheduled for that afternoon didn't take as long as expected, and he returned early and sat with Orphan on the front steps, scratching the soft, short fur between the dog's velvety ears while he listened to the industrious sounds of Lily's vacuum cleaner.

The dog still had a worried, anxious air about her, but already, in just one day, she'd calmed down a great deal and, in her own mournful way, seemed happy enough in his company now.

Inside the house, the sound of the vacuum cleaner stopped and Daniel's scratching fingers grew still. His hand tensed. All afternoon he'd been thinking about Lily. Tonight she would be sleeping in the spare room. They would be sharing dinner. Breakfast tomorrow. And the same again the day after. Was it fair to have her living here, cleaning his house while knowing next to nothing about him, wondering what the hell had landed him in jail?

The answer was hardly a brain-teaser. It wasn't fair to leave her in the dark. He knew that. But to actually talk about it all with someone who wasn't a policeman or a lawyer or a social worker felt like a quantum leap.

Until yesterday he hadn't been in the mood to talk to *anyone*, and it was damn amazing that he'd actually let Lily into his life. But there was something unstoppable about her.

What was also amazing was that Lily had been prepared to stay here. He realised, with something of a shock, that he knew as little about Lily Halliday as she did about him.

Her footsteps sounded on the veranda behind him, and he looked up. 'All finished?'

'Yep. That's the spare bedroom done and dusted.'

She stood near him, lightly resting a neat hip against a veranda post and crossing her arms as she looked down at the dog stretched sleepily beside him. 'Orphan's made herself at home.'

'Yeah. She seems to have settled in.'

'Are you going to keep calling her Orphan?'

Daniel's eyebrows lifted. 'Maybe. Orphan's a rather fitting name for such a sad-looking dog, isn't it?'

'Do you think she's sad-looking?' Lily reached down and tickled Orphan's ear. 'Did you hear what he's saying about you, beautiful?'

Daniel swallowed hard. What was the matter with him? Lily was tired, at the end of a hot day's housework, dressed in a cobweb-smeared T-shirt and faded jeans, and she was bending forward to scratch the dog's ear. Why the hell would that inspire his intense fascination? He felt heat tremble through him as he imagined her reaching out to touch him with that same easy confidence.

'Maybe we should give you another name,' Lily said to the dog. 'Something happy.'

Daniel swallowed again, and wondered if it was possible to feel so much desire for a woman and do nothing about it. Tempting fantasies of a hasty affair with this passing stranger had been haunting him all day. But what a damn fool idea that was.

Hell. Even if Lily was the kind of twenty-first-century girl who indulged in flings, he hadn't the right to make love to her. How could he taint her with his darkness?

He forced himself to think about the dog rather than the woman. 'What's a happy name for a dog?' he asked.

'Ooh, let me think.'

He hadn't really been serious, but clearly Lily was.

'"Joy", maybe?' she said.

'I guess.'

'Or what about "Felicity"? That means happy, too.'

He wrinkled his nose. 'I can't imagine yelling out to a dog called Felicity.'

'Well, no, perhaps not.'

Lily plopped down on the step beside him, close, almost touching, and he felt his blood begin to sizzle.

'What other names mean happy?' she mused. 'There's "Blythe", I suppose. Or "Hilary".'

Daniel shook his head. 'A station dog has to have a name that sounds good when it's yelled across three or four paddocks.'

She frowned at him. 'Can't you just whistle for her?'

'Yeah, but you still need a good name you can yell.'

'Well, that's easy to test.' Flashing him a cheeky grin, she hopped to her feet again, jumped two steps and jogged a short distance across the grass. Cupping her hands to her mouth, she tipped her head back and yelled into the afternoon blue, *'Jo-o-oy!'*

Daniel felt Orphan quiver in reaction to the raised voice.

Lily turned back to him, smiling broadly. 'How did that sound?'

'Not bad.'

He couldn't help grinning back at her. She was so lovely and untroubled and happy; she had an uncanny ability to dredge up big smiles from the murky depths inside him.

'Try "Sunny",' he said, letting his hand glide over Orphan's bony spine.

'Sunny? That's a good one.' Lily tipped her head back again, and the deep afternoon sunlight lent her tawny hair a golden sheen. '*Su-u-n-nee!*'

She flipped him another grin. 'Sunny rolls off the tongue more easily than Joy. "Smiley" would be nice, too.'

'Yeah. Smiley's good. I like that.'

This time Lily's eyes narrowed shrewdly as she looked back at him. 'Come on, then, it's your turn. Come and give Smiley a test-yell.'

Her laughing eyes challenged him. Innocently? Daniel felt like a kid again, challenged to a childish dare, but of course there was nothing childish about the vital, golden woman waiting on the lawn.

He glanced at Orphan, who was watching him with forlorn brown eyes. 'No need for a test,' he said. 'A dog that looks this sad is just asking to be christened Smiley.'

'Oh, come on, Daniel. Don't be a spoilsport. Come and yell it out to make sure.'

A cold, wet doggy nose pushed against Daniel's hand. He looked at Orphan's mournful eyes and then again at Lily's bright, smiling face.

This was crazy, he decided as he got to his feet and crossed the lawn. Crazy, but fun.

Standing beside Lily, he said, 'One yell coming up.' He let his head fall back, raised his hands to cup his mouth and let '*Smi-lee!*' ring out across the paddocks.

'Yes!' Lily cheered. 'Smiley sounds great.'

He found he was grinning. Again.

Behind them, on the steps, Orphan's tail was wagging. 'It works, doesn't it?' he said.

'Sure does. So you'll call her Smiley, then?'

He nodded. 'I reckon it's a terrific name for her.'

'Way to go!' Lily flung triumphant arms above her head, leaping high into the air like a cheerleader.

Her skin glowed in the afternoon sun, and the shiny river of her hair broke free from its clasp and bobbed on her shoulders. And, as her feet reached the ground again, Daniel felt a burst of genuine happiness deep in the pit of his stomach.

He pulled her into his arms.

And he kissed her.

Her lips had been parted in laughter, but the laughter died as his mouth met hers, and she went very still.

For a heartbeat he feared he'd made a fool of himself—that she was going to pull away from him. But she stayed. Oh, yes. She stayed.

She stayed, warm and soft and wrapped in his arms, and he kissed her slowly, tenderly and thoroughly. Savouring every delicious sensation.

The afternoon melted around him and he was no longer conscious of the dog or the homestead or the paddocks and the distant cattle. He was aware of nothing but kissing this sweet woman. This earthy, womanly woman.

He wanted to kiss her for a week, to go on kissing her till the world stopped.

Nothing else mattered but this happiness. This heart-lifting pleasure.

With Lily in his arms he could hold back the darkness… Indefinitely…

With Lily in his bed...

Daniel broke the kiss and stepped back, breathing hard.

Lily made a soft sound of dismay. Her eyes sent him a silent question, but she didn't move.

'That was—that was a thank-you,' he said. 'For Smiley.'

Her eyes were suspiciously bright, and she blinked rapidly. 'You're welcome.'

CHAPTER FIVE

LILY dumped her backpack on the bed in the spare room where she was to sleep, and yanked the zipper with such frantic energy that she almost broke it.

She. Felt. So. *Stirred.*

Daniel's kiss had left her shaken. Shaken to her roots. And scared. Yes, scared. It was very scary to realise that she could be so completely and gloriously reduced to a trembling mass of longing by one careless kiss.

And she was unbearably confused, too. Had there ever been a man so difficult to read? Daniel might as well have been a message written in Swahili, for all she could understand him. His kiss had been so unexpected, but so thorough and beautiful. And sexy! Oh, goodness, yes.

And then he'd had the effrontery to look as if he'd regretted it.

How dared he?

How dared he be so upset and distracted that he'd charged off with Smiley, muttering something about a windmill that needed attention?

Angry tears burned her eyes.

She was angry with herself as much as with Daniel. She shouldn't have let his kiss get to her. Hadn't she learned tough lessons about men? First from her father and later from Josh? Since then, she'd prided herself on never letting down her guard where her heart was concerned. She'd perfected the art of flitting from boyfriend to boyfriend like a carefree butterfly, determined to have fun and not to be hurt.

Plenty of other men had kissed her, and she'd found the experience pleasurable, but hardly life-threatening.

But with Daniel there'd been no warning. She'd been rendered helpless by his kiss—electrified by the potency and urgency of his mouth locked with hers.

She'd been overcome by a heady rush of wanting. Worse, she'd fallen—blissfully, giddily, thrillingly—smack on her face in love.

She'd been a fool—a fool to let such feelings get the better of her. And Daniel had looked dismayed when he'd realised his mistake.

What was wrong with them both? They were both adults, who'd been around the block more than once, but they were behaving more like inept teenagers.

Now, angry and emotionally drained, Lily flopped onto the bed. The mattress bounced and her backpack lurched, spilling some of its contents onto the bedspread, including a small drawstring bag.

Sobered instantly, she picked the bag up. She loosened the strings and tipped it so that three round, river-washed stones, painted in her father's signature gaudy colours, rolled out.

Marcus Halliday had painted this little rock family for her when she was four years old. And here they were still. She carted them with her wherever she went—a father, a mother and a little girl, with cheery, red-apple cheeks and bright beady eyes, and hair painted so meticulously she could almost see every individual strand.

How Lily had loved them!

She'd adored these stone people, and she'd adored her father for creating them for her. As a child, she'd played with them endlessly. They were her special gift from Marcus and later, after he'd left, they'd been her only link with him. Maybe if he'd never given them to her she would have adjusted more easily to his leaving. But he *had* given them, and she'd cherished them.

'I painted them especially for you and only you, sausage,' Marcus had told her. He'd always called Lily 'sausage', and she'd loved him for that, too.

Later, she'd hated him for leaving her, but back then, when he'd lived with Fern and her in the little house at Sugar Bay, Lily had adored him as only a little girl could adore her father. He was strength, he was safety, he was hugs. And love.

She had so few images to remember him by, but she recollected clearly the sight of his strong, sun-tanned legs coming in from the beach, his feet trailing sand on the floorboards as she crouched behind an armchair, suppressing excited giggles during a game of hide-and-seek.

She remembered the smell of his cigarettes, and how she would sit in his lap, and how he'd allowed her to flick his silver cigarette lighter...

But along with those happy memories came the pain, sharp, swift and cruel as ever...

There was a sudden knock at her bedroom door, and Lily jumped.

Daniel was standing in the doorway, watching her with worried eyes. She realised her eyelids were stinging, and she lifted a hand to touch her cheek, surprised to find it wet.

'You're upset,' he said, looking almost as unhappy as she must have looked. '*I've* upset you.'

Embarrassed to be caught crying, she couldn't immediately think of anything to say. She glanced down at the three cheery stone faces grinning up at her, and then hastily shoved them back into the drawstring bag, brushed at her cheeks with the backs of her hands and swung her legs over the edge of the bed.

'I'm OK,' she said, and with forced casualness dropped the bag into her pack and closed the flap.

When Daniel looked doubtful, she gave the backpack a careless pat. 'I've been having a pathetic moment, but it has nothing to do with you. It's just a little emotional baggage I should have offloaded years ago.'

He nodded slowly, then turned his attention to the door-frame, running a thumb over a deep scratch in the white-painted timber. His throat worked. 'I shouldn't have kissed you like that,' he said.

Lily sighed. 'Yeah, you made it perfectly clear it was a mistake.'

'I hope you'll accept my apology. It's not going to happen again.' He cocked his head towards her door. 'You won't need to put a padlock on your room.'

Good grief! How many ways was this man going to tell her that kissing her had been a bad idea?

Folding her arms over her chest, Lily eyed him angrily. 'Oh, come on, Daniel. I told you I wasn't upset about you. I'm not going to fold in a heap just because of one little kiss.'

He looked taken aback.

'You don't have a monopoly on bad memories, you know.'

Slowly, as if this was a new idea that was taking its time to sink in, he nodded.

Feeling bolder now, Lily decided to push her advantage. 'But perhaps if this arrangement is going to work, we need to get a few things out in the open.'

'What sort of things?'

'I think it would help us both if I knew what happened,' she said, and then nerves gripped her and she gulped. 'I know I said I didn't need details about why you went to jail. And I'm not trying to be a sticky-beak, but wouldn't it make things easier—for you—if I understood what you've been through?'

It was like watching a man turn to stone.

'I doubt it,' he said stiffly.

'I'm sure it must be very difficult to talk about,' Lily said more gently.

He shook his head with sudden impatience. She could see his anxiety rising—in the clench of his hands, the military-stiff tension of his shoulders, the tight line of his mouth. His eyes were cold and furious.

'I did time, Lily. Prison's not a place I'd recommend. But I wasn't beaten up by guards. I wasn't brutalised by my fellow inmates.'

'But it's left its mark on you.'

If possible, his jaw tightened even more. 'I'm not prepared to discuss it. What's the point?' He was almost shouting now. 'If I told you what happened, what, exactly, would you understand?'

Lily's mouth opened and shut like a landed fish. In the face of his sudden fury, she couldn't think of an answer. Dismayed, she dropped her gaze and fiddled with the zipper on her pack.

And then, from the doorway, she heard a deep, groaning sigh, and when she looked up she caught a fleeting glimpse of Daniel's darkly flushed and agonised face before he covered it with his hands.

She felt terrible. 'I'm sorry, Daniel,' she said. 'You're absolutely right. I couldn't possibly understand what you've been through—even if you tried to tell me. It's none of my business.'

Keeping her gaze averted, she desperately tried to change tack. She rummaged in her pack to find her toiletry bag and a change of clothes. 'Please, forget I asked. Would it be OK if I took a shower now? And then, if you like, I'll cook dinner.'

Daniel didn't speak, but he nodded, and then stepped back out of the doorway, turned abruptly on his heel and marched away.

As Lily pottered about the kitchen, preparing a simple meal of spaghetti Bolognese and salad, she could hear Daniel switch on the shower.

She was tired, physically and emotionally, but her mind, of course, would not let go of all that had happened that day— the discovery of the wedding photograph, Daniel's impulsive kiss, and then the final, upsetting exchange in her bedroom.

One thing was certain—from now on she was going to play it very carefully with Daniel Renton. An emotional distance was imperative. It was what he wanted. And it was sensible. Safe.

She'd been a fool to begin to care about him. She'd been even more of a fool to push her way into his life. But now that she was here she knew it would be best for both of them if she simply cleaned his house as quickly and as efficiently as she could and then left. Daniel would be better off without her.

The pub might have vacancies now that the weekend was over. At a stretch, she could afford to stay there for a few nights. Before she knew it Audrey would be back, and she'd focus on helping her mother. Fern was her priority—first and last. Actually…while Daniel was showering, it was a good time to put a phone call through to Sugar Bay… She dialled the number in her mobile phone.

'Everything's wonderful,' Fern assured Lily when she rang. But Fern always said everything was fine, no matter how much pain she was in.

Problem was, there was little point in trying to supervise a parent by remote control. Fern had lived by her own rules all her life and, unfortunately, she wasn't about to change.

'Don't hurry back,' she said, when Lily explained how long she would be away. 'You deserve a bit of a holiday. Have a great time, won't you?'

'Thanks. I'm—I'm sure I will.'

Lily suppressed a sigh. She hadn't told Fern why she was in Gidgee Springs. Her mother wouldn't have understood and certainly wouldn't have approved. Fern had never demanded from Marcus the money that was rightfully hers. She'd always insisted that money wasn't important—that the universe would provide. But the universe had never really come up trumps, and Fern had always lived hand to mouth. If she'd known of Lily's plan to get money from Audrey Halliday, she would have done her best to talk her daughter out of it.

So Lily's plan was to secure the money first and then find

a way to justify it to Fern… Audrey's generosity could be interpreted as the universe delivering the goods at last. Or karma. She would think of something.

All Lily knew was that it was up to her to look after Fern now. 'I'll ring you again soon, Mum. Take care, now.'

As she was hanging up, Daniel came into the kitchen.

'I was just ringing home,' she said, trying to ignore the little jolt in her heart when she saw him fresh from the shower with his hair still damp. 'Dinner's ready. Spaghetti Bolognese.'

'Smells wonderful.'

He said this lightly enough, but the tension that had flared before still lingered while they ate. Lily had tuned the kitchen radio to a station that played light pop. Music during dinner—even moody love songs—was better than moody silence.

'There's ice-cream in the freezer,' she reminded him as they finished their first course. 'Rum-and-raisin. Would you like some?'

Leaning back in his chair, Daniel considered this as he patted his taut, toned stomach. 'Rum-and-raisin ice-cream.' A slow grin emerged, surprising her. 'That's a temptation I can't resist.'

Pleased by this unexpected warmth, Lily heaped generous scoops into a bowl for him and gave herself a smaller helping. But their dessert didn't provide any magical sweetening of the mood. Daniel murmured appreciation as soon as he tasted the ice-cream, but they ate it in much the same manner as they'd eaten their first course, in silence, listening to the radio, with Smiley stretched on the floor between them.

'I'll do the dishes,' Daniel said, jumping to his feet as soon as he polished off the last creamy scoop.

'I'll dry,' Lily offered.

She could tell by the way he stopped in mid-stride that he was about to protest—to send her away. He stood in the middle of the kitchen with their empty bowls in one hand and the other hand resting lightly on his hip.

Lily waited, feeling silly—like a child in the playground hoping to be allowed to join in a game. 'Perhaps you'd rather I left you alone?' she suggested.

'No.' He let out an embarrassed, huffing little laugh. And then, after a beat, 'I've been alone for too long.'

His blue eyes met hers across the kitchen. Their gazes held, and her heart juddered as she realised that Daniel was letting her in.

I've been alone for too long.

She could see his vulnerability, unmasked. It was all there, in his eyes.

I've been alone for too long.

Daniel was offering her his fragile trust.

Her throat felt choked. Despite his efforts to keep her and the rest of the world at bay, this man needed people. He needed her.

The truth of it smote at her warm heart. She would give anything to be able to throw her arms around him, to tell him that the world was full of sunshine and there was some for him.

But that would be too much, too soon. *Softly, softly...* All he wanted—all he needed from Lily—was friendship.

For Daniel, the kiss was behind them—a minor road-bump to be forgotten.

The world, viewed through the kitchen window as Lily and Daniel attended to the dishes, was black. Clouds covered the moon and the stars, and Lily couldn't even see the distant light of another farmhouse.

'How far away are your neighbours?' she asked.

Daniel paused and looked out into the gloom. 'I used to be able to see old man Flynn's lights through there once, but the scrub's regenerated and it's much thicker now.'

'Does the old man live out here by himself?' she asked.

'Not any more. He lives in town now.' Daniel frowned as he enticed the last of the Bolognese sauce from the bottom of the saucepan.

'Did you worry about him when he was living alone?'

He flicked her a sharp, wary glance. 'You wouldn't be setting a trap for me, would you, Lily?'

'A trap? What on earth are you talking about?'

Daniel sighed deeply. He'd finished the washing up and was rinsing soap suds from his strong brown hands. As he stood watching the last of the bubbles disappear down the drain, he said, 'I know I'm going to have to tell you sooner or later. I guess it's best to get it over and done with.'

Lily stood, teatowel in hand, holding her breath. Once again she'd asked prying, unwelcome questions. It was on the tip of her tongue to tell Daniel he didn't have to tell her anything, but his next question distracted her.

'Where's that fancy coffee of yours?'

'Um…in the pantry.'

'How about you make some and I'll tell you my story?'

There was, of course, no need to ask which story.

Her stomach tied itself into nervous knots.

He managed a faint smile. 'You're dead right, Lily. I'll feel better if I get it off my chest.'

'OK,' she said softly, and as Daniel drew out a tall stool and perched on it she filled the kettle and fetched the coffee and the plunger.

He watched her for a bit, and then started abruptly, like a swimmer making a sudden decision to dive into icy water.

'Old Flynn was a sick and lonely pensioner, trying to scratch together a living on the property next door. His family never had time to visit, but they'd telephone from the city, try to talk him into moving into town so they wouldn't have to worry about him. But Flynn wouldn't budge.'

Lily, listening carefully, nodded as she poured boiling water over the coffee grounds in the plunger. Fern was just as stubborn. *'I won't leave Sugar Bay till they carry me out in a box,'* she'd said.

'So I used to keep an eye on him,' Daniel said. 'You know—a couple of times a week I'd call in for a yarn and a cuppa. Every so often I'd do some mustering or yard work there—keep an eye on his fences. But one time when I was over there I discovered the local thug, a bully called Briggs, hanging about the place, frightening the poor old bloke. Later, Briggs tried to coerce Flynn out of the few cattle he had left— he'd actually punched the daylights out of the poor old fellow.'

Daniel's face twisted with a dark emotion. Anger? Contempt? Horror? Lily couldn't be sure. A prickly lump troubled her throat.

'Briggs was a weasel,' he said. 'A mongrel. He already had a track record with the police.'

He paused, and Lily saw the pain in his eyes and the tension in his jaw.

'I suppose you can guess what happened next?' he said.

'You got into a fight. With Briggs. Trying to defend old Flynn.'

'Exactly.'

This was said with such harrowing regret that Lily felt her eyes fill with tears.

Daniel's eyes had become bleak chips of blue slate.

'Coffee's ready,' she said, and she pushed down on the plunger.

He nodded, and waited while she filled a mug and handed it to him.

'Thanks.' He took a sip, and released a soft sound of approval.

Then, as she sat at the table with her coffee, he said, 'I only gave Briggs a black eye the first time.' He paused and sighed heavily. 'But then the sneaky rat came from behind me with a tyre lever, planning to do me over. I had no choice but to hit him as hard as I could to defend myself.' Daniel shot Lily a tense, warning glance. 'Briggs hit his head on a metal picket on the way down.'

'Oh, no,' she whispered, too appalled to think of a more adequate response.

'It was one of those freak accidents.' He bared his teeth in a grimace. 'A freak *fatal* accident.'

Oh, God. Daniel had killed a man.

So much worse than she'd expected.

She felt sick. Sick for Daniel.

She couldn't help thinking of the gentleness of his hands as he'd examined the labouring heifer. He'd been so eager to save the calf's life. And he'd taken such care with the frightened dog she'd brought him. His gentle hands had held her while he kissed her…

It didn't really seem possible that the same hands that had delivered the calf and cradled her face had killed a man.

She knew this dreadful accident would have tortured him. It would go on torturing him for ever. No wonder he hadn't wanted to talk about it.

He sat very still on the stool, with the heels of his boots hooked over the rails, and clutched the coffee mug tightly as he stared with fierce concentration at a spot on the floor.

Watching him, Lily felt her heart almost break. Her head buzzed with a hundred questions. 'I don't understand,' she said. 'I don't understand why you had to go to jail. It was an accident, wasn't it? It was self-defence? Surely you're allowed to use reasonable force to defend yourself?'

'In most cases,' Daniel agreed, and then, without any prompting, he added, 'But, unfortunately, old Flynn passed out, so he wasn't able to be a witness. And Briggs's father suddenly arrived on the scene, and somehow, in the midst of all the confusion, the tyre lever mysteriously disappeared.'

A look of frustration twisted his face. 'The police searched everywhere, and they couldn't find the lever.'

Lily frowned. 'But Heath Drayton believed your story. He seemed quite confident you were innocent.'

Daniel nodded and took a deep sip of coffee. 'Couldn't get me off the hook, though.'

'So in court it was your word against the father's?'

'Yeah. Without the tyre lever to prove that I'd been attacked with a weapon, there was no way to justify why I'd used such force to thump Briggs a second time.'

He let out his breath slowly. 'In the end it was bad luck all round. It was election time, and the Attorney General was making a big splash in the press about demanding stricter, tougher sentencing. The local police talked the State Prosecutor out of a murder charge, but the district magistrate took the new ruling to heart. He was determined to send me down.'

'So what did you get?'

'Three years for manslaughter.'

'Three? That's so unfair!' Lily cried. How could Daniel have tolerated the undeserved humiliation, the injustice and the restrictions? It was too, too cruel.

'They let me out after eighteen months for good behaviour.'

'How—?' Her voice faltered and she had to stop, to draw a deep breath and try again. 'How could you bear it?'

He shook his head. 'Not very well.'

What could she say? She tried to put herself in Daniel's shoes, but her imagination was too limited by her own safe world. Her mind shrank from accepting the grim reality that had been a daily occurrence for this gorgeous man. What chilling memories haunted him?

Setting her coffee cup aside, she stood and walked to him, and rested her hand lightly on his forearm. 'Daniel, it's over. It's all behind you now.'

'Yeah.' He sighed. 'I keep telling myself that. One day I'll believe it.'

He set his cup on the draining board and straightened, pushing back his shoulders and drawing in a deep breath. He looked pale, as if the task of telling his story had drained him completely.

'I'm ready for bed,' he said, confirming this.

But as he crossed the kitchen Lily sensed a lightness in his bearing. He seemed less burdened.

In the doorway, he stopped and looked back. His blue eyes looked deep into hers and he said, very simply, 'Thanks, Lily.'

It was like being touched by a flame, the tail of a shooting star.

CHAPTER SIX

By THE end of the following day, Lily had decided she'd really lifted her act as a housekeeper. She had dusted and vacuumed and polished the dining room to within an inch of its life. She'd wiped down the walls and the ceiling, and she'd washed the lacy curtains and hung them on the clothesline in the back yard to dry. And when she'd brought them inside they'd smelled exactly the way washing powder commercials promised—of lemons and sunlight and fresh air.

She'd also brushed and scrubbed the walls on the front of the house, and swept and hosed down the veranda and its railings. She'd even managed a quick trip into Gidgee Springs to shop, and now the fragrant aroma of chicken and lentils spiced with cumin was wafting through the house.

'I'm a domestic goddess,' she announced to the empty house with a chuckle.

As she showered and changed into clean clothes, she heard Daniel's voice calling from outside in the hallway.

'Hey, something smells great.'

He sounded happy, and her heart did a crazy tap-dance.

All day she'd been trying to put yesterday's kiss out of her mind. And on each of the four or five million times she'd remembered how heavenly it had felt to have Daniel's mouth locked with hers, she'd reminded herself that the kiss had been a spur-of-the-moment impulse. Afterwards he'd made it blatantly clear that he regretted the mistake.

And perhaps her efforts to curb her growing obsession might have worked if she and Daniel hadn't shared that intimate conversation after dinner. How could she not feel emotionally involved with him now?

Thing was, she had no idea how *he* was feeling. He'd been gone all day—working on one of Ironbark's distant boundaries—so she hadn't been able to gauge his mood. Now, she felt ridiculously nervous.

In the bathroom mirror, she saw a sudden rush of colour in her cheeks, almost as deep as her crimson T-shirt. *Fool.*

She quickly ran a comb through her damp hair, straightened her towel on the rail, took a deep breath and opened the bathroom door.

Daniel was standing just outside, dressed in his working gear. His shirt was crumpled and dusty, his face streaked with sweat, and his jaw shadowed with dark stubble. But he was—in a word—breathtaking.

'I—' She passed her tongue over lips that were suddenly dry. 'I guess you'd like to use the bathroom? I've just finished.'

He didn't answer straight away. He simply stood there, looking at her, letting his eyes travel slowly over every detail of her appearance—from her damp hair hanging loose about her shoulders, to her halter-neck red T-shirt and white jeans, to her bare toes with their pearly pink nail polish.

His Adam's apple moved up and down in his throat.

And Lily literally couldn't breathe. Thoughts of his kiss filled her head. The memory of it teased her lips. It shimmered alive in the air between them.

A strangely strangled sound, a cross between a gasp and a sigh, escaped her. 'If you'll let me past,' she said, in little more than a whisper, 'the bathroom's all yours.'

Slowly, too slowly, he stepped to one side, and Lily edged past him. She could smell the not unpleasant mix of dust and manly perspiration that clung to his clothes, and she felt a shocking need to stay right there in the narrow hallway, almost touching him. Almost… Almost…

'Did you go for a swim today?' she asked.

Fool! She'd been thinking too much about his body. *What a dumb, dumb question.*

Daniel grinned. 'Yeah. Smiley and I both had a cooling dip in the river around noon.'

Quickly she hunted for a change of topic. 'I—I hope you didn't have anything special planned for dinner?'

'Nothing that would smell as good as what you have cooking.'

'I—thought I'd save you the trouble.'

'Great thinking, Lily.' He smiled lazily. 'I like the way you think.'

The terrible thing was, Lily was quite sure Daniel knew *exactly* what she was thinking. And he knew it wasn't about dinner.

Again, she felt a need to moisten her lips. 'Dinner will be ready in about twenty minutes. I'll—um—just be setting the table.'

She turned and fled to the kitchen.

The table took two minutes to set, and Lily found herself pacing nervously.

'How silly is this?'

Smiley, watching from a corner, wagged her tail, and Lily consoled herself that at least one member of the household was becoming more relaxed. Smiley might not have lost the anxious and haunted look of a war refugee, but she had come ahead in leaps and bounds as a tail-wagger.

We need music, she decided, but not the radio tonight. She went through to the living room. She'd already checked out Daniel's CD collection when she'd dusted this room. He had a rather extensive mix, covering everything from heavy metal back to the folk groups of the sixties. There was even some opera. She chose something soothing, but just a little moody.

And then she went back to the kitchen and stood at the sink, looking out at the bush. A kookaburra was perched on a fence-post, its beady eye fixed on something in the grass. A light breeze fluttered the pink feathery tops of the grass at the edge of the track, and the kookaburra swooped, then took off again with what looked like a lizard in its beak.

Nearby, in the home paddock, the red heifer grazed while her new calf slept at her feet.

'Oh, so you've set the table in here?'

Lily spun around at the sound of Daniel's voice. He'd shaved and changed into clean stone-washed denim jeans and a white shirt. He looked drop-dead divine.

A sweet pang pierced her chest, and she had to cling to the edge of the sink. *Oh, heavens, I'm in love with him.*

Daniel was frowning at the seersucker tablecloth and the blue and yellow china she'd set on the table.

'Is something wrong?' she asked.

'I reckon this meal tonight deserves something a little better than the kitchen. And, as you've done such a great job on the veranda, why don't we eat out there?'

He smiled. Gorgeously.

Was it her imagination, or was there something new in his voice? Almost as if he'd made a conscious decision to put the darkness of his past behind him this evening. Perhaps last night's confession really had helped him. The thought excited her as she began to gather up the things on the table.

Daniel stopped her with a hand on her wrist. 'Let me look after this.' In an easy movement, he hooked a chair in each hand and carried them out onto the veranda, set them beside a cane table. Then he disappeared into the dining room and emerged with a white tablecloth. Soon he'd added silver cutlery and his best, elegant china—white, edged with gold.

'Oh, wow! This is lovely. We should have candles and flowers, too.'

He scratched his head. 'I suppose there must be candles here somewhere.'

'I think I saw some in the sideboard in the dining room.'

While Daniel went in search of candles, Lily hunted in the weed-tangled garden and found three creamy gardenias.

'Perfect,' Daniel said, when she placed the flowers on the table between two tangerine candles in glass holders. They stood looking down at the elegant table they'd created, and the gardenias' sensuous perfume drifted up and around them.

'All we need now is the food and wine,' said Lily.

'And sunset. Followed by moonlight.'

'Yes.' Her heart leapt into her throat, and she couldn't help wondering where all this was leading. Was it merely a pleasant meal? Or something more? She was intensely aware of Daniel, of the way he looked, of his every movement.

In the kitchen she took the casserole from the oven and carried it outside. She heard the clink of glasses and the pop of a cork as Daniel opened the wine she'd brought on that first night. Music drifted through the open French doors, and down near the creek curlews sent out their haunting calls.

The veranda was bathed in the golden light of sunset. The candles glowed like little warm home fires. Everything looked so romantic, and she felt strangely light-hearted. Happy.

They sat, and Daniel poured wine into their glasses. 'I spent long, long months dreaming about sharing a lovely meal like this, out here on this veranda,' he said.

Her throat tightened at the thought of all the meals he'd had on the prison farm, day after dreary day, for eighteen long months. 'Here's to good times ahead, Daniel.' She touched her glass to his.

'Good times indeed.'

They tasted their wine—a full-bodied South Australian red—rich and mellow.

Daniel looked at her. 'It's time to make amends.'

'What for?'

'You have to admit I haven't been the easiest to get along with.'

His sincerity flustered her. 'Don't worry about it. It's understandable…all things considered.' She lifted the lid of the casserole pot and warm cumin-and-chicken-scented air rose between them. 'Are you ready to eat?'

'Absolutely.' He sniffed appreciatively. 'That smells amazing.' And then, as he tasted the food, 'It *is* amazing. This is sensational, Lily.'

She tried not to look too pleased.

They talked about Ironbark, and Lily learned that three generations of Daniel's family had lived on this property, that his parents were quite elderly now and had moved to Brisbane, where his older brother lived.

'I'm surprised your family didn't look after the property for you while you were away,' she said, trying not to sound too shocked by their lack of support.

He shook his head. 'Mum and Dad are too frail now, and my brother's just not interested. He actually urged me to sell up. He offered to invest any profits in the stock market.'

'How kind,' Lily said, doubtfully.

'Bill was trying to do the right thing, but he doesn't understand how I feel about Ironbark, and he doesn't see its massive potential. If I ever get this place back to its full carrying capacity, it'll bring bigger returns than any investment he's ever made.'

'What does your brother do?'

'He's a dentist.'

'A dentist? Did he grow up here with you?'

'Until we went to boarding school. He fell in love with the suburbs—couldn't wait to have a neat brick home, with a neat little wife, a rotary clothesline and two-point-four kids. Bill's never looked back.'

Lily looked out at the extravagant sunset and the purple hills, the peaceful, lavender-tinged paddocks, and choked back a laugh. 'He gave up a chance to live here, like this, to stare down people's mouths and drill teeth?'

'As fast as he could.'

They exchanged bright glances of mutually amused disbelief.

'It takes all types,' she said.

Daniel sent her a sparkling, skin-crinkling smile.

Oh, man—when he decided to smile properly, he pulled out all the stops. Suddenly overcome, she dropped her gaze. She let a small piece of chicken slip to the floor for Smiley, and watched the morsel disappear in one blissful doggy gulp.

Daniel lifted his glass again, but paused with it halfway to his lips. 'Now it's your turn,' he said. 'I want to hear about you, Lily. Tell me about Sugar Bay. How long have you lived there?'

It was a revelation to discover how pleased she was that Daniel wanted to know.

'I was born in the bay,' she told him. 'I went to school there, but there weren't many jobs for young people, so I moved to Sydney when I was eighteen.'

He seemed surprised. 'Why Sydney? It's a long way from home.'

'I was restless. You know how it is when you're eighteen. Far-away places seem more exciting. And I knew a guy from the bay who'd already moved there.'

'A boyfriend?'

'Yes.' To her amazement, she was able to speak about Josh without the usual accompanying lurch of her heart.

'So…how did you take to life in the Big Smoke after the peace and quiet of Sugar Bay?'

Looking up, she saw that Daniel was watching her carefully, and she sensed a sudden alertness in him, almost as if her opinion of Sydney was important. Why? What did Sydney mean to Daniel?

'I loved it,' she told him honestly. 'I was lucky enough to share a flat in one of the beach suburbs, and my boyfriend Josh helped me to find my first job—working in a video store. Once I found my feet, I got a job with a community radio station. Then I signed up for a part-time course in photography and scored a job on a suburban newspaper. A couple of years later I had a really lucky break—hitting the big time with a job on a fashion magazine.'

'As a photographer?'

'Mmm.' She nodded and sipped her wine.

'So, what happened to the boyfriend when you went to Sri Lanka?'

She shrugged carefully. 'He was ancient history by then. Already moved on to greener pastures.' Wow! She'd actually said that without a wobble.

'And the job?'

'I had to resign.'

Daniel's eyebrows lifted high. 'That's a tough call.'

'Not really. Not for a girl who's grown up in the bay. When I saw the terrible damage after the disaster in South-East Asia, I couldn't bear it.'

'A lot of people couldn't bear it, but you took action, Lily.' He said this gently. 'That's pretty special.'

She shrugged again, and ate a forkful of lentils.

Daniel leaned forward, eager to make his point. 'Most people are moved by terrible disasters. And a lot of us have good intentions. But we don't actually down tools, give up secure jobs and rush over there to help.'

'Other people don't have a role model like mine.' She drank some more wine. 'Fern, my mum, has spent her whole life helping others—delivering their babies, taking them food when they're sick, giving them a bed when they've nowhere to sleep. I guess that sort of thing rubs off on you.'

He sent a glance along the veranda. 'So, all this is your mother's fault?'

'All what?'

'My beautifully clean house.'

'Oh? Well, yes. You can blame my mother for all my bad habits. Without her influence I would never have barged in here, taken over your house and turned it into a showpiece of rare and distinguished beauty.'

They both chuckled.

After a bit, Daniel said, 'You're very close to your mother?'

Lily nodded. And then she pictured Fern as she'd seen her last, looking too tired and in too much pain, barely able to walk, and she sighed heavily.

'Something the matter?'

'My mother's not well.'

His eyes were instantly shadowed with concern. 'That's a worry for you.'

She tried to make light of it. 'Fern would insist she's OK. It's just a bad hip—nothing life-threatening—just incredibly painful.' She looked away to the last of the sun—a thin golden line along the distant tops of the hills—and she wondered if it was her turn to confide.

'I'm afraid she'll need a wheelchair before too long,' she said. 'And her beach cottage has tiny rooms, uneven paving and misshapen doorways. It's going to be totally unsuitable. But she's like your old neighbour. She won't hear of living anywhere else.'

'It's a dilemma, isn't it?'

'It would all be solved if she had a hip replacement. Actually,' Lily added, 'Fern's problem is the reason I'm here.' It was best that she told him everything. 'I'm waiting to meet with someone on Friday. Someone I hope can—can help.'

'Someone out here?' He couldn't hide his surprise.

'A—a family connection. Audrey Halliday. She was married to my father.' She paused briefly. 'Marcus Halliday.'

'The artist? The guy with the big house overlooking the river bend?'

'I haven't been to his house, but that sounds like the sort of place he'd like.' Her hand tightened around the stem of her wine glass, and she set it down for fear she'd break it. 'Marcus died a month ago.'

Dismayed by the tremble in her voice, she said brightly, 'But I don't want to get into all that this evening. This is an important celebration.'

He considered her for a thoughtful moment, and then, to her relief, he seemed to accept her lead.

'Absolutely.' Lifting the bottle, he topped up their glasses.

By the time they'd finished their meal and the wine, night had fallen. The CD had stopped, the birds had gone quiet, and the only sound was the occasional thump of Smiley's tail and the muted buzz of insects in the grass.

And, in the midst of the peacefulness, a question that had been building and building inside Lily for the past twenty-four hours—twenty-six and a half hours to be exact—simply begged to be asked.

She tried to ignore it.

But after the mellow wine and the chummy conversation,

and the intimate mood on the veranda, she found its pressure irresistible. Like an erupting volcano, it burst from her.

'Daniel?'

'Yes?'

'Do you really think it was a mistake to kiss me yesterday?'

As soon as the question was out, she felt foolish. *Was it a mistake to kiss me?* That sounded so dumb. How old was she? Twelve?

What she should have asked Daniel was whether he would like another serving of rum-and-raisin ice-cream. Sick and shaky inside, she began to gather up their plates and cutlery.

'What are you doing?'

'Clearing the table,' she said, without daring to look at him.

'Why?'

Her head jerked up. 'Because—because these plates are—' There was a disturbing light in his eyes. 'To make room for dessert,' she finished lamely.

'But you asked me a question. Don't you want to hear the answer?'

Her mouth opened and shut.

Daniel stood slowly. 'If these dirty dishes bother you, let's move away from here.' He nodded towards a spot near the veranda railing—just out of the reach of the candles' light.

Lily rose, and her knees became so suddenly weak she almost fell over. Daniel took her hand and held it lightly as they walked away from the table. He leant a casual hip against the railing and kept her hand in his.

He looked down at her fingers, curling around his, and her heart went crazy, like a bee in a bottle.

'Was it a mistake to kiss you?' he asked, and his voice

was honey-smooth and molasses-dark—and her insides went into meltdown.

Could he possibly understand how she felt about him?

He raised his other hand to brush her earlobe with his finger, and she decided he knew exactly how she felt. He knew she wanted to drift closer, to curl into him and to feel his lips claim and possess hers.

But then, without warning, his hands dropped away and he turned from her and stared out into the night.

No!

Was he going to tell her again that the kiss had been a mistake? She didn't think she could bear it.

'I was selfish, Lily.' His voice took on a flat, world-weary tone as he stared ahead into the darkness. 'I kissed you yesterday for all the wrong reasons.'

Her heart seemed to slip from its moorings. How could Daniel change from being so confident and relaxed—and *seductive*—and now, suddenly, be so stern and remote? *Again?*

'Daniel, please, you don't—'

'I kissed you,' he continued relentlessly, as if he needed her to know the worst, 'because everything about you drove me to.'

She had a shadowy view of his gorgeous profile, and she saw the muscles in his throat clench, let go, and clench again.

'You drive me wild,' he said softly. 'The way you fix your hair fascinates me. The warmth in your eyes touches me, deep inside. There's so much joy and beauty in you, Lily, and I—I wanted some of it for myself.' His voice cracked, and he had to take a deep breath. 'I couldn't help it. I'm sorry.'

'Daniel—' Her own throat was so tight her voice emerged

as a croak. 'For heaven's sake, don't be sorry.' She swallowed and blinked. 'I'm flattered—really flattered.' She took a step closer. 'I'm not exactly in the habit of quizzing guys after they've kissed me, but if I had been I'm sure no other man could have offered a lovelier answer.'

He turned to her. His face was still in shadow, but she could see the glittering brightness in his eyes. She reached for his hands and felt them tremble at her touch. 'And, if you still feel that way, I'd really like you to kiss me again.'

She lifted his hands to her cheeks.

His fingertips caressed her. 'You're burning,' he whispered.

Of course she was burning. She was burning with anticipation. If Daniel didn't kiss her, she might explode like a firecracker.

But to her dismay he wrenched his hands from her again and stood staring down at them. She saw that they were shaking. Daniel was shaking. And he was staring at his hands with an expression of stark pain and horror.

After what felt like ages, he lifted his gaze to meet hers, and she saw the true depth of his pain—such a cruel pain— a pain that he didn't deserve.

'You—you know what these…' He turned his hands palms down, and she saw strong veins standing out against his suntan. Then he turned them palms up again, and she saw work-toughened calluses. He continued to stare at them. 'You know what these hands have done.'

Her heart almost broke for him. 'They defended a helpless old man.'

She interlaced her fingers with his, and together they stood, looking down. In the shadows and flickering candlelight her hands looked slender and pale against the darkness and roughness of his—like the moon inside clouds.

Heart thrumming, she dipped her head and pressed a kiss against the inside of his right wrist, and then his left. She kissed his palms.

'Lily.' His whisper was a warning, a choked plea for her to release him.

She shook her head slowly. And once again she took his hands and guided them—to her shoulders this time. Heart racing, she moved closer, praying that he wouldn't push her aside. Her hips settled against his, and she heard the sharp inrush of his breath.

The pads of his thumbs touched the bare skin at her collarbone, and every cell in her strained for more.

'Your hands are beautiful, Daniel,' she told him in a heated, husky whisper. 'And I want them. I want them all over me.'

A muffled groan broke from him, and for one heart-shattering moment she thought that now, at the last moment, he was going to walk away from her and leave her to drown in humiliation and misery.

But then, at last, he cupped her face, and she saw the nakedness of his hunger and the need in his eyes. He drew her swiftly to him, and his mouth covered hers, and she let the last of her worries dissolve.

Moonlight bathed Lily as she lay in Daniel's bed, too excited and moved to sleep.

Tonight's lovemaking had been the first time in a long time for both of them, and they'd stumbled into this room, feverish and fumbling, wanting everything at once—to touch and to be touched, to kiss and to cling, to shed their clothing and to plunge headlong into the maelstrom of passion.

But after the first obsessive, fiery conflagration they'd lain still in each other's arms, letting their breathing return to normal and the mad beating of their hearts slow. And then they'd taken their time.

They'd made leisurely, lingering, sensuous love, sharing deep, deep kisses and languid, teasing caresses.

Lily had never experienced such blissful, honest intimacy. And afterwards she and Daniel had held each other, with hearts so happy and full that they'd both had tears in their eyes.

And she knew that, whatever course the rest of her life might take, she would never forget this exquisite, magical night.

CHAPTER SEVEN

It WAS mid-morning when Lily opened the last of the closed doors in Daniel's house.

She'd tried another door first, but it had been locked. She'd had to go hunting until she found the key, hanging on a hook in the kitchen, and she'd opened the door to discover a desk with a computer, a telephone, a fax machine and walls lined with filing cabinets, as well as shelves of folders bulging with papers.

It had to be Daniel's office, and she hadn't liked to start cleaning there without consulting him first. So she'd moved on to the next room—the last room.

As soon as she opened it she knew there was something very important that Daniel still hadn't told her.

This was a child's room—and, despite the dust, the pony-print fabric used for the curtains and the bedspread, everything about the room, screamed *girl!* Lily stood gripping the doorknob as she took it all in.

An ancient pink dolls' bed in the corner was piled with dolls and teddy bears and other assorted stuffed toys. A collection of pennants, ribbons and certificates for prizes in pony club events hung on the side of the wardrobe. A rose-coloured

china tray on top of the chest of drawers held an assortment
of hairclips, pins, bead bracelets and ribbons.

The titles of the books crammed on the bookshelf showed
a high proportion of stories about ballet schools, pony clubs
and princesses. The little wooden table beside the window had
probably served as a homework desk, and was painted pale
green. And above it there was a cork board covered with
pictures of ponies. There was one with the name 'Grasshopper' printed carefully in green and purple crayon, and there
was a calendar from two years ago. And a photograph of five
little girls aged about eight or nine.

Lily crossed the room to look at the photo more closely. It
had been taken on the front veranda of Daniel's house, and the
girls were gathered around the same cane table she and Daniel
had used for dinner last night.

In front of one of the girls sat a fat birthday cake, decorated with pink icing, blue writing and yellow flowers with
mint leaves. A cluster of pastel-coloured candles had been lit,
but they were too close together for Lily to count them.

The girls were laughing, especially the one in the middle—
a slim, pretty child with shoulder-length dark hair and sparkling, familiar blue eyes. She looked so much like Daniel she
had to be his daughter.

Shocked, Lily looked around the room again, searching for
more clues. She picked up a book from the bookshelf, opened
it, and saw, listed on the flyleaf in a childish hand:

Jessica Renton.
Ironbark Station.
Via Gidgee Springs.

North Queensland.
Australia.
Planet Earth.

Lily's chest squeezed tight. She set the book aside and selected another, and then another and another. They nearly all had Jessica's name inside. And then she found one with an adult's handwriting:

To dearest Jess, with a mountain of love from Daddy, on your ninth birthday.

It had been dated—March, two years ago.

Lily felt so sick she sank onto the edge of the bed. A little girl, who looked like Daniel, had lived in this house, had slept and dreamed in this room. She *had* to be Daniel's daughter.

But if Daniel had a daughter where had the poor child gone while he was in jail? And where was she now? Why hadn't he rushed to collect her as soon as he'd been released? Why hadn't he mentioned her?

Her fingers traced the outline of a pony on the bedspread. She pictured Jessica Renton living here, going each day on the school bus to the sweet little school in Gidgee Springs, having friends home on weekends for sleepovers, learning to swim in the river, going to pony club on Saturday afternoons, happy and secure, with Daniel as her father. Together. A little team.

Until…

Daniel had gone to prison.

While he'd been away, someone must have cared for

Jess—either a relative or the State. But Daniel was home now. Why wasn't Jess here, too? Surely he hadn't abandoned her? Not Daniel!

She could not believe it!

Daniel swam strongly across the river, striking the water's smooth surface with powerful over-arm thrusts. He felt happy, happier than he had in a long, long time.

And it wasn't simply because he'd had sex last night. Lily had given him so much more than her body. In the past few days he'd felt the huge black shadow that had weighed him down begin to shift. He'd felt, at last, a glimmer of hope that at some time in the future the dark burden would slip from his shoulders completely and he would be free at last.

His whirling arms smashed the water. *Free. Free. Free.*

And it was Lily he should thank.

Open-hearted, loving, generous Lily—who, by some weird and wonderful twist of fate, had stumbled onto his property and into his life—was a gift from the gods. And he—poor, blighted fool—had done his best to turn her away, to throw her back.

Thank heavens for her tenacity.

He reached the far bank and turned, striking back the way he'd come, revelling in the cool, buoyant water.

Near the bank again, he paused briefly to reassure Smiley as she watched him, and then he turned again, swimming on, his mind toying with brand-new thoughts—so different from those that had tormented him most days when he'd swum here.

He wondered what Lily's plans were. He knew she was

worried about her mother and would want to get back to her. But was it possible that, at some time in the months ahead, Lily might want to come back here? Could he expect her to want to hang around on an Outback cattle property? Cara had hated it here, but Lily was different…wasn't she?

Daniel surged on, more strongly than ever, buoyed by an unfamiliar sense of optimism. Finally, he left the water. Time for lunch.

He stood for a moment on the bank and looked back at the river, watching its surface grow calm again now that he'd left it. He stooped to scratch Smiley's head, and she wagged her tail and gave small doggy noises of appreciation.

Crouching beside her, he hugged her and let her give his shoulder a loving lick. 'Thanks, mate.'

A couple of days ago he would have been certain that this was all he needed—his home and a dog, man's best friend. He hadn't dared to entertain fantasies about the future. He hadn't wanted to think about the long, dreary days ahead of him. But now he couldn't help dreaming about the remote possibility of a smooth and happy, ongoing relationship with Lily.

Even the eventual possibility of having Jess home again.

No, he was jumping the gun. It was foolish to try to think too far ahead.

He stood slowly, stretched his exercised limbs, and drank in the languid stillness of the afternoon, the sun's drying warmth on his naked body. Then he crossed to the bundle of clothes he'd left on the riverbank.

And, as he bent to grab his jeans, he saw Lily sitting in the shade of an acacia tree.

She dropped her gaze, but she knew it was too late to pretend that she hadn't been taking a good, long look at Daniel naked. In spite of last night's intimacy, she felt her face flame.

'What are you doing here?' he called.

'Waiting for you.' She kept her eyes lowered, but was intensely aware of his rough movements as he dragged on his jeans. It wasn't till she heard the rasp of a zip that she looked up, and her heart seemed to leap, then hang in mid-air.

He looked just as he had on the day she'd first met him, with his sculpted muscles glistening in the sun, his dark hair wild and wet, his faded jeans riding low on his hips—but today, instead of sending her a dark scowl, he looked halfway between stunned and delighted.

'How did you get here?' he asked.

'I walked.'

'You walked? It's five kilometres.' His eyebrows lifted high. 'How did you know I was here?'

'I took a guess.' She tried to smile, but it didn't work. She was too nervous. All morning she'd been consumed with anxiety and curiosity about Daniel's daughter. Why hadn't he brought her home? The problem was, calmness and common sense deserted her when she came head to head with the subject of fathers abandoning their daughters. Her own hurt and pain got in the way.

She'd been worried that Daniel might not return to the house till late in the day, and she'd known she'd burst if she had to wait till then. So she'd simply had to come to find him.

She patted the handle of the basket beside her. 'I knew you must be hungry, so I brought your lunch. Curried-egg and lettuce sandwiches, and a Thermos of tea. And a lemon cake.'

He grinned. 'A lemon cake?'

'It's a Greek recipe. I found it in a magazine. I poured warm lemon syrup over the cake as soon as it came out of the oven. I hope it's good. The recipe sounded delicious.'

'I'm sure it is.' Shirt in hand, he came towards her slowly, smiling uncertainly. He was watching her cautiously as he lowered himself beside her. 'Is something the matter?'

Damn. He must be able to sense how uptight and nervous she was.

'I hope not,' she said. 'But I did find something this morning…' She felt a moment's panic, and couldn't think of the right way to introduce the subject of Jessica.

Daniel frowned. 'What? What was it?'

She handed him a round of sandwiches wrapped in greaseproof paper. 'I opened the last door, Daniel. Not your study. I thought it might be best if I talked to you about that before I tried to clean it. So I went into the other room—' She paused, took a hurried breath. 'The little girl's bedroom.'

'Oh, yes,' Daniel said faintly, not meeting her gaze. With an excessive lack of haste, he set the packet of sandwiches on the sandy ground near his knee. 'That's Jessica's room. I—I meant to explain.'

Lily ran an anxious tongue over her lips. 'Is Jessica your daughter?'

'Yes, she most certainly is.' His intense blue gaze studied her.

Lily flushed and shook her head, but then she had to ask, 'Where is she, Daniel?'

His jaw squared defensively. 'She's living in Sydney with her grandmother.'

'Why?'

'Isn't it obvious? You know where I've been for the past eighteen months.'

Lily plucked at a stalk of grass. 'But why didn't you bring her home with you? Why isn't she here now?'

'She's better off at her grandmother's.'

In one angry, swift movement, Daniel leapt to his feet. 'For heaven's sake, Lily, what's got into you? Why so many questions? What would you know about this?'

'Quite a bit, actually.'

Astonishment froze Daniel. He stood, open-mouthed, hands on hips, staring down at her.

'I—I know how Jess feels,' she said, and all at once her face crumpled like a child's and she burst into tears.

He was crouching beside her in an instant, his hands on her shoulders, holding her.

'I'm sorry,' she spluttered.

'It's OK.' His voice soothed her; his hands gentled her as he rubbed her arms.

Lily sniffed. 'I told you I had emotional baggage. Well, here's the evidence. It catches up with me when I least expect it.'

'So what's this about?'

'Lingering issues—to do with my father.'

'Marcus Halliday?'

She nodded. 'He left my mother and me when I was five, you see. And I adored him. I couldn't believe it when he left. I never really got over it. I—I never forgave him.'

'Never?' Daniel had turned quite pale beneath his tan. 'But you still had your mother, didn't you? Aren't you and she close?'

'Yes. But my feelings for her have never been as complicated and deep as they were for my father. I'm not sure why.

Perhaps because she was always there. She wasn't a mystery. Marcus was obscure. And glamorous. Splendid, really. Larger than life. And he painted little stones for me. A little family.'

'Stones?' As Daniel settled onto the grass beside her, he raised a sceptical eyebrow. 'That was a big deal?'

Lily allowed herself the luxury of a childish pout. 'Those little stones happen to be the most significant present I've ever received.'

'Right.'

'Which only serves to prove how hung-up I am.' Her lips curved into a rueful smile. 'I know I should have got over him long ago. And it was wrong of me to draw comparisons. Jess's situation is different from mine. Totally.' She shot Daniel a hasty glance. 'Isn't it?'

'Totally,' Daniel said, but he didn't sound convinced.

Lily sat, hugging her knees, and he sank back onto the grass and lay with his hands stacked beneath his head, staring up through the criss-cross of acacia branches to the pale afternoon sky.

Both seemed to have forgotten the picnic lunch.

'I decided Jess was better off staying with her grandmother,' Daniel said at last. 'I wanted to protect her.'

'What from?'

His mouth thinned into a bitter downward curve 'From the stigma of having a criminal for a father.'

'Daniel, you were never a criminal.'

'I might as well have been. The results were the same. Jess still had a father in jail, for God's sake.'

He stared at the sky, and Lily, sensing there was more he wanted to say, waited.

'But I—I don't really know how Jess felt about it,' he admitted at last. 'Her grandmother kept her away from the trial. From everything. And Susan's convinced Jess is still better off in Sydney, well away from me.'

'How does Jess feel about that?'

Daniel closed his eyes, and Lily wondered if he was holding back tears.

'I don't know,' he said.

'You haven't telephoned her?'

He shook his head.

Carefully, she asked, 'You got on well with her before, didn't you? Before you went away?'

His eyes flashed open and he glared at her. 'Hell, yeah. We were great mates.'

'And you're missing her?'

'Oh, yeah.' He sighed heavily. 'The thing is, eighteen months in the clink kind of wrecks your confidence. I feel as if I don't have any rights any more—certainly not to mess with my daughter's life.'

Lily couldn't bear to see the pain in his face. She watched a line of tiny ants making their way towards her picnic basket. 'For what it's worth, I think Jess is probably missing you desperately, Daniel.' Smiling bravely, she leaned towards him. 'Just look at you.'

He eyed her with puzzled dismay.

'Maybe the fact that you're a drop-dead gorgeous guy impresses me more than it does Jess, but even if you weren't hot-looking you'd still be a truly wonderful man. And I reckon you're about as perfect a father as any little girl could be lucky enough to have.'

A derisive, croaking laugh broke from him. 'Get real, Lily.'

'It's the truth,' she said, smiling as she poked at his broad, bare shoulder with her finger. 'And I'm willing to bet that, no matter where you've been, or what bad things you've experienced, Jess still believes in you.'

He stared at her, listening hard, and then, very deliberately, switched his attention to something in an overhead tree branch. Lily's heart picked up pace. She felt suddenly terribly nervous, but she also felt an urgent need to get through to him.

'You're the only father Jess has, Daniel. And I'm almost certain that a day doesn't pass when she doesn't miss you, when she doesn't long to hear from you. She's been separated from you for too long. She needs to be home, here at Ironbark, with you, Daniel—sleeping in her little bedroom at the end of the hall, getting to know Smiley. Most of all, she needs to hear you tell her that you love her.'

He looked up at her, his eyes bleak, his mouth twisted with the effort of keeping his emotions in check. 'I'm—I'm very much afraid you're right.' He blinked hard, and a tiny muscle in his jaw went into spasm.

Lily's heart broke for him, and her eyes refilled with tears. Leaning over him, she dropped a gentle kiss on his pulsing jaw, and then another on his lips.

Then she tried to draw away, but his hands prevented her. He cradled the back of her neck, holding her in position above him so that her lips couldn't leave his, and he returned her kisses with a hunger that tore at her heart and left her aching. Breathless for more.

'Lily,' he whispered hoarsely, and he wrapped his strong

arms about her, drawing her down against his broad, bare chest. 'Oh, God, Lily, I need you.'

She had no power to resist him.

With the sun on her back, and Daniel's warm, glorious body beneath her, his open lips were heaven and she was a willing prisoner in his arms.

'What's going to happen to us?'

As soon as Daniel asked that question, he felt a cold chill, like a premonition. He and Lily were in the living room after dinner, relaxing on the sofa with coffee and ginger chocolates. Lily had her feet up, and it was all very comfortable, all very cosy.

'What would you like to happen to us?' she asked.

He let his head drop back against the back of the sofa and pretended to give this some thought. 'I guess I'd like a replay of this afternoon…on a daily basis.'

Lily smiled. And he smiled, too. And their smiles were laced with intimate memories of this afternoon, when they'd made love on the shady riverbank. And afterwards…when they'd discovered they were ravenous and they devoured Lily's curried-egg sandwiches and cake and washed it down with tea from the Thermos flask.

And then Lily had suddenly declared that she wanted to swim.

'You'll get cramp,' Daniel had insisted.

'Pooh. That's an old wives' tale. I grew up at the beach, remember? I've proved it wrong a thousand times.'

And so they'd swum. But Lily had rejected Daniel's habit of ploughing back and forth from bank to bank. She would have none of that. She'd wanted fun—the kind of fun she believed the river was meant for, and that Daniel had almost forgotten. She'd wanted to dive and frolic like a playful dolphin. She'd wanted laughter. And to make love in the shallows.

And then, near sunset, they'd driven home together, showered together, cooked dinner together and eaten it together.

Daniel had never known a woman so at ease with herself, at ease with him and at ease with his lifestyle. Lily held the shadows at bay. She made the world OK again, and made life worth living.

But now he needed to talk about the future.

'You'll be heading off soon.'

'Yes, on Friday.' She chewed at her lower lip. 'Once I leave here I don't expect I'll be able to see you again for quite some time.'

He nodded, and tried not to look too disappointed. 'So, let me get this straight. You're going to visit your father's second wife. What's her name again?'

'Audrey. Audrey Halliday.'

'And you're hoping she will help to finance your mother's surgery. Is that right?'

'Yes. I don't really know what my chances of convincing her are. But even if I'm successful, and the surgery can be scheduled soon, it'll be some time before Fern's fit enough for me to leave her. And if I can't get the money…' Her eyes took on an unexpected vulnerability. 'If I can't get the money I'll have to get a job and take care of Fern for as long as she needs me.'

Reaching out, he took her hand and gave it a squeeze. 'You're a very persuasive young woman. I'd say your chances of getting the money are very high.'

'I hope you're right.' Sitting straighter, she curled her feet beneath her. 'What about you, Daniel? Are you going to Sydney to beard that lioness of a grandmother in her den?'

'Yes. Of course I'll go to battle with Susan if I have to. I really want Jess back here.'

He watched for her reaction to this, and was rewarded by a radiant smile.

'I hope she'll want to come with me.'

'She will, Daniel. I'm sure of it.'

He drained his coffee, and they sat for a while in contemplative silence until he said, 'While I'm in demon-facing mode, there's something else I want to do.'

Lily lifted a curious eyebrow.

'I'm going to pay a visit to Mick Briggs,' he said.

She gasped. 'The father? The jerk who hid the tyre lever?'

'Yes.'

'Why would you want to visit him? I'd have thought you wouldn't want anything to do with him. It was his fault you went to jail. He committed perjury.'

Jail. Perjury. The words brought feelings of panic. Darkness loomed towards Daniel. His throat constricted.

'I need closure,' he said loudly. Loudly enough to send the gloom scattering.

Lily considered this with a thoughtful frown, and then nodded slowly. 'He might not welcome you.'

'I'm damn sure he won't. But I can't let that put me off. The idea came to me this afternoon, in the middle of our conversation about fathers and Jess and how I feel about her. I suddenly understood the grief and pain that made Briggs react the way he did. I thought about losing Jess, about how I would feel if another person took her life—

even accidentally—even if she had done something very wrong. And I—' He hesitated, unwilling to put the feeling into words.

'It's a thought beyond bearing,' Lily said gently.

'Yes,' Daniel agreed, immensely grateful that she understood. 'When I was in court, I expressed regret for my actions, but I've never said it to Briggs—man to man. As one father to another, I've never asked for his forgiveness.'

'That would be an incredibly noble gesture, Daniel.'

His shoulders lifted in a faint shrug. 'I have to do it. Otherwise this dark feeling will stay in me for ever.'

Uncurling her legs with the lissom ease of a cat, Lily knelt on the sofa, leaned forward and kissed him lightly on the lips. 'You're a very special man.'

Then she settled companionably beside him, and he put an arm around her shoulders and dropped a kiss on the top of her head. It seemed incredible that he'd only known her a few short days. In many ways, the best ways, it felt like a lifetime.

'Perhaps,' he said, thinking aloud, 'I should go to Sydney this week—maybe tomorrow? Then you would still be here, and you could meet Jess when I bring her home.'

Lily's brow furrowed in a pensive frown. And he realised he shouldn't have voiced that thought. He'd presumed too much. Asking Lily to meet Jess suggested a longer-term relationship—something they hadn't discussed.

Casually, in an effort to generate a different slant on the subject, he said, 'I know Jess would really like you.'

Lily pulled a wry face. 'She might not, you know.'

His eyes flashed incredulity. 'Of course she would.'

'She might see me as competition for your attention.' Lily

frowned again as she considered this. 'Actually, when I think about it, I'm sure it would be best if I was out of the way when Jess comes home. She's going to have enough to deal with, just settling back here. Going back to school here, and everything. She doesn't want some strange woman hanging around, making sheep's eyes at her father.'

'Or sleeping in his bed.'

She sent him a sparkling, sexy glance. 'Exactly.'

They kissed again, and Lily tasted of ginger and chocolate—sweet and spicy and everything sexy. A soft, happy, hungry groan escaped Daniel.

Their kiss was luxuriously unhurried—as languorous and lazy as a summer afternoon—and somehow, in the middle of it, Lily managed to end up curled in his lap with her arms entwined about his neck.

He still couldn't quite believe the miracle that this lovely, loving woman wanted him.

After a while, when they broke the kiss, Lily made herself comfortable, lying with her head in his lap.

Daniel ran his fingers through her silky hair and tried to tell himself that all would be well after she left. He'd bring Jess back to Ironbark. Jess would fill his life for now—Jess and Smiley. He'd get Jess's pony, Grasshopper, back from the friends who were caring for it. And with Jess home he would be forced to get involved in the local community once more. He would be busy. Normal.

But…

He traced the line of Lily's cheek. But Lily would be gone. His heart began a fretful sort of beating.

She smiled up at him. 'Don't look so sad.'

'I hate the thought of losing you when I've only just found you.'

'You're not going to lose me. I'll be back. In case you haven't noticed, Mr Renton, I'm quite, quite taken with you.'

His lips slanted into a shaky grin.

'Actually,' Lily said, 'I think the correct word is "smitten".'

'Smitten?' He touched her hair, looped a tendril around his little finger. 'Yep. I'd say that describes me, too. I'm definitely smitten.'

'I might even be in love,' Lily suggested shyly.

Love. The word seemed to hit Daniel smack in the solar plexus. He felt exhilarated. On top of the world. And scared.

He'd tried *love* and failed abysmally.

Lily was looking up at him, watching him carefully, and suddenly she looked embarrassed, as if she would happily drop through a crack in the universe. She swung quickly out of his lap and into a sedate, upright position. 'Forget I said that.'

'Why?'

'I shouldn't have mentioned it—*love*. It's a four-letter word.'

'But it's a four-letter word that's quite acceptable in polite company.'

She smiled uncertainly.

'Just the same,' he said. 'I must admit—after my attempt at marriage—my faith in the happy-ever-after kind of love has taken a nosedive.'

'Yeah. I had a boyfriend and a father who made me wonder, too. You find yourself asking if the real thing, the whole till-death-us-do-part scenario, isn't just some big con-trick.'

But, in spite of her cynical comment, Lily's eyes were luminous. She gave a little shake. 'Anyway,' she said, as if she was determined to stay upbeat, 'isn't absence supposed to make the heart grow fonder?'

'So they say.'

'So you and I have something to look forward to.'

He smiled.

'And in the meantime…' Lily reached down to the coffee table and helped herself to another piece of chocolate. 'In the meantime, there's chocolate.' She popped the smooth dark cube into her mouth, and ate it with obvious sensuous delight.

'In the meantime,' corrected Daniel, snaring her hand and bringing her chocolate-smeared fingers to his lips, 'we have the rest of this week.'

'Yes.' Her reply was a husky whisper, and she shivered with delicious delight as he nibbled and licked chocolate from her fingertips.

Trailing her tongue along her lower lip, she said, 'Daniel, I think there's a little more chocolate here.' Her eyes were lustrous with a sense of fun, and something far deeper and more intimate.

'We can't have that,' he said, drawing her into his arms. 'Let me take care of it.'

It was raining on Friday morning, when it was time for Lily to leave, so they said their farewells on the veranda, almost needing to shout over the downpour drumming on the iron roof.

'Drive carefully,' Daniel warned. 'There are creeks all around here, and they can fill very quickly.'

'At least I'll have plenty of petrol,' Lily said, managing a smile, but not a very happy one.

He nodded, and shoved his hands in the back pockets of

his jeans, wishing he had a photographic memory. He wanted to remember her just as she was now, dressed in jeans and a pink-and-blue-striped shirt, with her thick, wavy hair caught back in a loose braid, her eyes bravely bright and determined.

'Good luck in Sydney, Daniel. You've got my address and phone number. You will let me know how things go with Jess, won't you?'

'Sure.' Daniel tried to say more, but an embarrassing croak emerged. He cleared his throat and tried again. 'Good luck to you, too. I really hope everything works out for your mother.'

'Thanks.'

He kept his hands stuffed in his pockets, too afraid that if he touched her he would want to haul her close and never let her go.

He looked out at the thick curtain of rain pouring down. 'Maybe you should wait until the storm's passed.'

'No, I've already waited too long. I've got to get this over with. Audrey's expecting me.' Bending, she extracted a small tartan drawstring bag from a pocket in her backpack and held it out to him.

'What's this?'

'Hold your hand out,' she said, as she loosened the drawstrings.

Frowning, he dragged his right hand from his pocket and held it palm upwards.

Three stones fell from the bag. One rolled, and he quickly caught it with his left hand.

'Well saved,' she said, and then she bit her lip.

'Are these your stone people?'

'Yeah.'

Three little round faces looked up at him—faces full of character. A wide-eyed man, a gentle-faced woman, and a gleeful little girl with thick fair hair.

'I thought I'd leave them here for Jess,' she said.

He shot her a sharp glance. 'Are you sure?'

'Absolutely. But don't worry if she doesn't like them, or if she feels too old for them. It doesn't matter. You can throw them away if she doesn't want them.'

'I promise you I won't do that.' He turned them over, recognising in the simply painted, almost comical faces the artistic genius of Marcus Halliday. The stones were probably worth a small fortune. 'Do—do they have names?'

She blushed. 'I used to call them Marcus and Fern and Lily. But Jess is welcome to call them whatever she likes. Or not. As I said, I don't mind if she's not interested.' Her chin lifted a fraction higher. 'I don't need them any more.'

He knew this decision could not have been made lightly. He was almost certain there was a deeper symbolism behind Lily's gesture, as if she were casting off things from the past that had weighed her down. Just as he had to do.

A sudden sparkle of tears in her eyes confirmed his suspicions, and he felt a rock-like obstruction in his throat.

She stepped back quickly. 'I'll be off, then.' Her voice was tight and matter-of-fact. She stooped and grabbed her backpack by the shoulder straps.

'Let me carry that for you.'

'No, thanks. I've got it. I'll be fine.'

This wasn't a moment for kisses or tender farewells. Neither of them could handle that.

'See you when I see you,' she said.

He nodded. 'Best of luck, Lily.'

'You too. I'll ring you when I have some good news.'

With a brief wave of her hand, and a curt, slanted smile, she lifted the backpack high and held it over her head instead of an umbrella, then turned and hurried down the steps and into the rain. And when she reached her car she didn't look back.

CHAPTER EIGHT

'DANIEL! Good heavens. How unexpected.' Susan Mainwaring stood in the doorway of her immaculate North Shore home, her agitated fingers plucking at the double string of pearls at her throat. 'What brings you to Sydney?'

'Three guesses, Susan.'

Her painted mouth pulled into a sour twist, as if she'd swallowed something extremely unpleasant. 'You should have telephoned to let me know you were coming.'

'I was afraid you would find a reason to stop me.'

She pretended to be affronted, and then glared at him with open hostility. 'I suppose you're hoping to see Jessica?'

'Of course.'

'I'm afraid she's not here. She's still at school.'

Daniel adjusted the cuff of his long-sleeved city shirt and checked his watch. 'It's after four. She'll be home soon, won't she?'

'Not today.' It was announced with undisguised triumph. 'Jessica has hockey practice on Tuesdays.'

'Today's Wednesday, Susan.'

'That's what I meant. Wednesday. Yes, silly mistake. Hockey practice is always on a Wednesday.'

'I'm happy to wait for her.'

'I suppose you are,' she said unhappily, and she sent a frantic glance towards her neighbour's windows as if she was suddenly afraid someone might see her with this unsavoury character on her doorstep.

'It's been a long time,' Daniel reminded her. 'Too long. I have to see Jess.' He offered Susan his most charming smile. 'But I don't mind if she's a little late; it gives us time to talk.'

'Talk?' she squeaked.

'I'm sure there are things we need to discuss before I take Jess back to Queensland with me.'

'Daniel, you can't. For God's sake. Be reasonable.'

There was a flick of the curtain at the neighbour's window. Daniel turned and waved to the woman peeking there, and she promptly vanished.

Susan gasped.

'Don't you think it would be better if we discussed this inside?' he said.

When she didn't reply, Daniel took two steps forward, and she stepped back into the hallway.

'You can't turn me away, Susan.'

Looking pained, she lifted a hand in a half-hearted flourish, indicating that he should enter.

'Wait here.'

Daniel waited, as she'd ordered, in the middle of her hallway. Glancing past her, he could see through to the lounge, and he thought he caught a movement reflected in the mirror on the far wall.

'Do you have a visitor?'

'No!' Backing towards the lounge with her arms splayed on either side, Susan looked like a basketballer in defence, trying to block his way.

'Who is it, Grandma?' called a girl's voice.

Jess!

An adrenaline rush, violent as a lightning strike, coursed through Daniel.

'Jess?'

His little girl was in there? His heart thrashed against the wall of his chest. He took a step towards Susan, and she raised a shaking hand to halt him.

'Jess is here,' he hissed, through gritted teeth.

Susan began to shake her head, but she stopped. Her eyes were almost pleading. She opened her mouth, and then shut it and pressed her fingers to her lips.

He stared at her carefully painted fingernails pressed against carefully painted lips. 'I want to see my daughter.'

'Dad?'

And suddenly Jess was there, in the doorway behind Susan, looking impossibly tall in a navy blue school uniform with a starched white collar and dark stockings, and shiny black shoes. Her dark hair had been cut short into a neat bob that curved elegantly in to her jawline. She looked so grown up—so different from when he'd last seen her, eighteen long months ago.

But it was Jess, *his* Jess.

Her mouth dropped open when she saw him. She stood ramrod-still, her blue eyes huge, immobilised by shock. And then her face contorted into a wobbly smile. Her eyes sparkled with sudden dampness. 'Daddy!'

'Hello, Jess.'

Jess was shaking, and then she began to cry. Daniel's vision blurred, but somehow he stumbled past Susan. And then his daughter was in his arms, clinging to him, hugging him hard.

All his pain, all his longing, crashed over him. Holding her tightly, he felt sobs heave in his chest. Oh, God, he'd missed Jess so much. And here she was at last—his little girl.

His emotions were in tumult. He felt so buoyed up by the joy of reunion, and yet shattered by the instant realisation that he'd paid a dreadful price. His little girl was so grown up now, almost a stranger.

His tears blinded him. He was shaking. All he could do was hold Jess against his chest and hug her close.

'I didn't think I was ever going to see you,' she whimpered. 'I missed you so much, Daddy.'

'I know, chicken, I know. I missed you, too.' He stroked her sleek, neat hair. 'I missed you so much, baby. Every day.'

They shared watery smiles. Daniel traced her soft cheek with nervous fingertips. 'You're so pretty.'

'Grandma said you weren't coming. But deep down I've been hoping.'

'I've come to take you home.'

'Home?' She looked up at him, her eyes shining through tears. 'Home to Ironbark?'

'Yes.'

'You mean that? You're not kidding?'

'No, I'm home for good now, and I want you there with me, Jess.'

'Oh, wow!' Jess let out her breath on a huff of excitement. 'Oh, *wow*!' She jigged up and down with delight. 'I can't believe it. That's so excellent. I've missed everything about home. I've missed you. I've missed Grasshopper. My friends.'

'Oh, dear,' Susan cried behind them. 'Oh, dear.'

Jess pulled a small distance out of Daniel's arms, her face anxious as she looked at her grandmother. 'What's the matter, Grandma?'

'I'm going to lose you,' Susan cried, dabbing a white linen handkerchief to her eyes.

Daniel saw Susan's tears, and the confusion in Jess's face, and felt his throat constrict. Throughout his marriage Susan had been a manipulative pain in the backside, but she loved Jess. He had no doubt of that. The poor kid was torn by conflicted loyalties.

But Daniel was quite certain he knew what should happen here. Lily had helped him to see that. He was Jess's father. In a just world, he and his daughter would never have been separated. And now he'd come to claim her back.

'Jess,' he said. 'Your grandmother and I haven't had a chance to talk about this. Do you think you could give us a few minutes alone?'

Jess tightened her hold on Daniel. She glanced in Susan's direction, but then her eyes locked with Daniel's, and she seemed to sense his determination to take charge.

'Would you like me to make some tea?' she asked.

Daniel swallowed his surprise. His little girl made tea? 'Yes, thank you,' he said. 'That would be lovely.'

'Is that all right with you, Grandma?'

Still dabbing at her eyes, Susan nodded. 'Of course, dear.'

Jess smiled at them both, stood on tiptoes and kissed

Daniel's chin, and then hurried to her grandmother and kissed her cheek before dancing in the direction of the kitchen.

In the doorway, she paused and turned back. 'Dad?'

'Yes, Jess?'

'What's it like at home?'

He caught the wistful note in her voice, and his heart ached for her. He knew just how she felt. They'd both been in exile for far too long.

'Ironbark's much the same,' he told her. 'The river's still got plenty of water in it. But the land's overgrown and weedy. I've got a lot of clearing to do. A—a friend helped to clean up the house, though, so it's pretty good.' And then, as an afterthought, he added, 'I have a new dog.'

She beamed at him. 'What sort?'

'Just a mongrel—a kelpie-collie cross. We called her Smiley.'

'We?' Jess's expression grew tense, her eyes sharp and wary. 'Is someone else living there with you?'

'Not any more, Jess. But there was a woman who—there was a friend—the one who was helping. She's gone home now.'

Jess accepted this without further comment and, sending them another quick smile, she disappeared.

Daniel and Susan sat.

'You've taken wonderful care of Jess, Susan,' Daniel said. 'I really am very grateful. For everything.'

'She means a great deal to me.'

'And to me.'

Over the coffee table, their eyes met, and the light of battle glinted in Susan's.

'I know you love her,' Daniel said carefully. 'And I understand, too, that Jess is an important link to Cara for you. I have no intention of cutting you out of Jess's life. But—' he paused significantly '—but you must accept that I'm her father. You went out of your way to convince me that Jess was better off staying on with you, that you're the best person to bring her up. Not me. I've decided I can't possibly agree with you. My daughter should live with me now.'

Susan sat very straight in her chair, with her hands carefully folded in her lap. Now that her silly attempt to hide Jess had been exposed, she was a figure of dignity.

'There are things you need to accept, Daniel,' she said. 'The most important is that Jess is very happily settled into school here now. Given the difficult circumstances, it took some time for her to make new friends, but at last she's happy.'

'I'll admit that shifting her from school to school is not ideal,' Daniel said, just as firmly. 'But Jess is still young. She has another year after this before high school. I think she'll adjust.'

Susan cocked her head to one side and eyed him shrewdly. 'You've changed.'

He thought of Lily, and felt a rush of gratitude and happiness. 'Yes, I think I have.'

'Is a woman involved?'

Shocked that she'd arrived at that conclusion so quickly, Daniel was momentarily lost for words.

'I'm right,' said Susan. 'There *is* a woman in the picture, isn't there?'

He mimed a seesawing action with his hand. 'Early days.'

Susan studied him a little longer, and then set her shoulders back, straighter than ever.

Daniel leaned forward, hardly daring to breathe. He could

see her mind working fast, and he prayed he could get through this without a messy confrontation.

At last Susan said, 'I do believe you deserve some happiness, Daniel.'

Another shock—even greater than the last.

'You're a decent man, and you've had some terrible unfairness in your life.'

'That—that's kind of you to say so, Susan.'

'I'm sure you know I wasn't happy when Cara married you. I didn't like to think of her stuck in the Outback with no life to speak of. But I have to admit you were good to her.'

She looked down at her manicured hands, now clenched tightly in her lap. 'I've had to live with the painful knowledge that if I had not interfered in your marriage Cara might never have left you.' Her mouth wobbled, and she had to take a moment to gather control. 'If I'd minded my own business, my daughter might still be alive. And Jess might still have a mother.'

Abruptly, she stood and turned from Daniel, and, like a grand dame of the stage about to deliver a meaningful line in a play, she fixed her gaze on a spot above a vase of pink and white lilies and pressed one hand against the pearls at her throat. 'Daniel, you're right. You should take your daughter home.'

He jumped to his feet. 'Thank you,' he said, hardly daring to believe they'd reached this point.

'I'll miss her terribly, of course.'

'I know. I promise Jess will keep in touch.'

Susan looked at him then, and she managed a small, wavering smile. 'Perhaps she can come to visit me sometimes in her school holidays.'

'Of course.'

'And you should encourage her to write letters.'

'I will.'

An uneasy silence descended, and Daniel toyed with the idea of making a hasty escape before Susan changed her mind, or issued further demands.

It was almost a relief when a chirpy voice called, 'You guys finished, yet?'

Once more Daniel's and Susan's gazes met, this time without hostility. They nodded silently, acknowledging that the thing was settled.

Daniel said, 'Yes, we're finished.'

Jess popped her head around the corner. 'Is everything OK, then? Am I going home?'

'Of course you are, darling,' said Susan, with a careful smile.

'Excellent.' Jess beamed at them. 'Who's ready for a perfectly made cup of Earl Grey tea?'

Lily sat on the smooth, sun-warmed rocks below Fern's cottage and looked out at Sugar Bay. She'd always loved this view, with the white gulls circling over the sparkling water and the boats dancing whenever gentle waves rocked them at their moorings. But today she took little notice of the bay. Her thoughts were somewhere else entirely.

She was thinking about Ironbark, with its sleepy river, cool and inviting beneath over-hanging paperbarks. She was picturing paddocks dotted with cattle, and Daniel's homestead and its majestic backdrop of green-clad mountains, the cassia tree with its carpet of fallen pink blooms. She thought of Jess's room and the care she'd taken when she'd cleaned it.

Daniel might be back from Sydney by now. Was Jess with him? She would try to telephone him again this evening. She was desperate to know how things had gone.

They'd only spoken once since she'd got back, when she'd phoned to tell him the good news that Audrey Halliday had been surprisingly co-operative.

Unlike Fern.

Lily sighed as she remembered her mother's disappointing reaction when she'd arrived home with a generous cheque to be paid into Fern's account. Fern had looked so genuinely shocked that Lily had feared she might faint.

'Sit down, Mum,' she'd said. They'd been in the garden, overlooking the beach, and she'd pointed to a wooden bench nearby. 'Don't get yourself upset.'

'I'm all right, dear,' Fern had protested. 'But you've got to explain this. What would I need with all that money?'

'Mum?' Lily had gaped at her. 'You know perfectly well why you need it.'

Fern fingered a wisp of grey hair that had blown across her eyes. 'Oh…the operation.'

'Well, of course it's for the operation. Now we'll be able to get you an appointment with that nice Dr Peel in Brisbane straight away. He said he'd find a place for you on his list.'

Fern looked out to sea, and a gust of wind sent her long, silvery hair flying over her face. Lily couldn't see her expression, but she felt suddenly ill.

'Fern Mooney, you are *not* going to be silly and refuse to have this operation. I won't hear of it.'

Bracing herself with her stick, Fern bent stiffly forward to pick a stem of lavender from a bush growing through the fence, and lifted it to her nostrils. 'I'd be beholden to *that* woman,' she said quietly.

'Not to her. To Dad. And he's gone now, so you don't have to feel beholden to anyone. Dad should have given you that money years ago. You know that. Audrey knows it. That's why she's giving it to you now. Anyway, it's only a tiny fraction of all she inherited.'

'So you went to see her? When you were out west, you went begging?'

'Only because you won't ever ask for anything,' Lily cried, growing alarmed. 'All your life you've gone without. It was OK to be a martyr while you were young and healthy, but now you really need the money.'

If only Fern could be a little selfish. Just once.

In recent years, Lily had come to her own conclusions about why her parents' marriage hadn't worked. Marcus was ambitious and driven, and Fern, hating the idea of a life in the limelight, had simply stood back and let him take off for the stratosphere without her.

Fern sighed. 'You've always been impossibly spontaneous, Lily.'

'Please, Mum, don't do this to me. Dr Peel is so confident. He says you'll be a new woman. You'll be free to really enjoy your golden years.'

Fern raised her bony hand and stroked Lily's cheek. 'This operation has always been more important to you than it has to me.'

'But you will have it, won't you? Think of the alternative— getting more and more crippled. Being bedridden. All the pain.'

Fern dismissed this with a shake of her head.

'If you won't think of yourself, have the operation for me, then,' Lily pleaded. 'And for—for your grandchildren.'

'Grandchildren?'

'Theoretical grandchildren.'

A wistful smile played across Fern's face, and her eyes danced. 'What a delightful incentive. Do you have a theoretical father in mind for these theoretical children?'

'Only in—in theory.' Lily blushed. 'But don't get sidetracked. You *will* have this operation now, won't you?'

Fern's eyes remained sweetly wistful. And hopeful.

Lily held her breath.

Looking out at the curve of white sand and the azure waters lapping it, Fern said, 'I must admit, I hate the threat of that wheelchair.'

'Just think. You'll be able to stay in this house. You'll be able to garden again, and go for long walks along the beach. You can go swimming and snorkelling.'

'It really was very kind and brave of you to go to all that effort for me, Lily. I'm being an ungrateful wimp, aren't I?'

'Yes,' Lily agreed gently. 'But you're going to be sensible now, aren't you?'

Fern smiled. 'All right. I'll do it.'

Lily had been so relieved, she'd almost cried as she hugged her mother. Now, as she sat lost in thought, she heard her mother calling her name, and she turned to see Fern standing at the dilapidated paling fence that separated her cottage's garden from the beach.

Fern was leaning heavily on her walking stick, while her loose cotton dress flapped about her in the breeze, and Lily winced at the thought of the effort it had taken for her to leave the house. Each step must have been agony.

Thank heavens Dr Peel had been true to his word. Fern's operation was scheduled for next week.

Leaving the rocks, Lily hurried up the beach.

'There was a phone call for you,' Fern called.

Lily thought of Daniel, and her heart skipped a beat. 'Who was it?'

'A man called Daniel Renton.'

Lily kicked at the rickety gate to free it from a tangle of goat's-foot creeper and straggling grevillea bush. 'What did he say?'

Fern shook her head and laughed. 'I'm afraid I couldn't get anything out of him except that he wanted to speak to you. I told him I'd have to find you, and that I'm a bit slow and shaky on my pins, so he's ringing back in ten minutes.'

'Right.' Lily's heart was pounding. She was desperate to speak to Daniel. Ten minutes felt like a lifetime.

She helped her mother back into the house. 'I'll make a cup of tea,' she said, and began quickly to fill the kettle at the sink.

'I haven't met this Daniel Renton, have I?' asked Fern.

'No. I—I met him while I was out west. In the Gidgee Springs district.'

Lily set the kettle on the stove, and took a deep breath. What was the matter with her? She was so jittery she could hardly manage to light the gas.

Fern's eyes were thoughtful and alert as she watched her daughter. 'I think Mr Renton said something about a person called Jess,' she said.

'Jess? Really?' In the process of reaching into an overhead

cupboard for mugs, Lily froze. 'That—that's his daughter. Did he say whether she's at home with him?'

'I'm not sure, darling.' Fern's mouth curled in a wry smile. 'But I think you should forget about making this cup of tea and get straight on the phone to him. I presume you have his number?'

'Yes.'

Fern's eyes glowed. 'Off you go, then.'

'OK.'

Lily went through to the sitting room and perched on the edge of Fern's ancient couch, which was draped with vibrant Indian saris and scattered with gaudy cushions. Fern's phone was the old-fashioned kind—black and square—and it involved dialling the numbers rather than pressing buttons.

'Hello, Ironbark Station.'

It was a girl's voice, bubbling with lively and youthful enthusiasm. It had to be Jess.

Lily pressed a hand against a sudden beating in her chest. She'd been so sure Daniel would answer. But how silly to be nervous of his young daughter.

'Is that Jess?'

'Yes. Who's speaking, please?'

'This is Lily, a friend of Daniel's,' she said. 'Could I speak to him?'

'Hang on. I'll just get him.'

Thirty seconds later, Jess was back. 'Dad's taking the call in his study.'

She said this, Lily noted, with a marked loss of enthusiasm.

Daniel was on the line almost immediately. 'Hello, Lily?'

And then there was a click as Jess hung up.

'Hello, stranger.'

'Hey, there.'

With just those two words she could tell that he was happy, and she felt her face stretch into a broad grin.

'It's so good to hear your voice,' he said. 'How are you?'

'I'm fine, Daniel, and I'm so pleased Jess is home with you. Did that go well?'

'Amazingly well. I've got so much to tell you.'

'I'm sure you must have. I'm all ears. Fire away.'

Settling back into the soft, deep cushions on the couch, she listened to Daniel's low voice with its lazy Outback drawl as he told her about his trip to Sydney and his return home with Jess.

'She's so happy here,' he said. 'She and Smiley have really hit it off. It's a match made in heaven.'

'That's a bonus.'

'You wouldn't believe the change in that dog.'

'So she's no longer anxious and cowed like a pitiful refugee?'

'Not at all. She's mischievous and cheeky. Practically a puppy again. The change in such a short time is bordering on miraculous.'

'And Jess is really happy, too?'

'So far, so good. I got her pony back, and she's taken him through his paces, and that went well. She goes back to school here on Monday. That might be a bit of a hurdle.'

'Have you had a chance to talk to the teacher?'

'I've got an appointment before school, Monday morning.'

'You're going to have your hands full now, trying to run the property and manage being a father, too.'

'Yeah.' He let out a sound that was half-laugh, half-sigh.

'I had this fabulous housekeeper, but she's taken off and left me in the lurch.'

'Silly woman,' Lily said, trying hard now to keep her voice light. 'Do you think you'll try to get another housekeeper?'

'I reckon I'll keep the position vacant for a bit,' Daniel drawled. 'The old one had a lot of potential, so I'm hoping to entice her back here.'

Smiling into the phone, she hugged a cushion to her chest. 'She'll probably come if you offer a good incentive.'

'Hmm,' he murmured sexily. 'That's food for thought.'

They both chuckled, and Lily could feel their mutual desire like a live thing, pulsing down the phone line.

And then Daniel said, more soberly, 'Just before I left for Sydney, I went out to the Briggs place.'

'Really?' She gripped the phone tighter. 'How did it go? I bet he was shocked to see you.'

'He certainly was. When I first got there, he wasn't going to let me in the house. He started yelling abuse, brandishing a rifle, and threatening to run me off the place.'

'Daniel! For God's sake! What did you do?'

'Stood my ground. Eventually the message sank in that I wasn't leaving until I'd said what I'd come to say.'

'And it worked? He listened?'

'Yeah.' He paused. 'I knew he'd be taken aback and embarrassed when I started talking about apologies and forgiveness.'

There was a stretch of silence, and Lily sensed that Daniel was having a battle with his emotions as he tried to recount what had happened.

He cleared his throat. 'Mick broke down,' he said. 'He'd

been carrying a lot of guilt, I guess, and—and in the end he actually apologised to me.'

'Oh, Daniel.'

Thinking about it, Lily felt her own emotions tip out of balance. She pressed a hand to her mouth to hold back a sob.

'That—that's wonderful,' she said at last. 'It's what you needed to hear. I'm so pleased. I wish I could give you a hug.'

'You and me both, Lily.'

They talked more of the nonsense that only lovers shared, and then they talked about Lily's plans for the trip to the Brisbane hospital next week with Fern. Eventually they hung up, with fervent promises to keep in regular touch.

As Lily set the phone down and got to her feet, she noticed a mug of tea on the coffee table. Fern must have hobbled into the sitting room and left it there, and Lily hadn't even noticed.

She picked the mug up and discovered with surprise that the tea was stone-cold.

Jess didn't look up when Daniel came into the kitchen. She was sitting at the table with a plate of tomato sandwiches that she'd already begun to eat. Another plate, piled high, was set in Daniel's place and covered with a clean tea-towel.

'I was starving,' Jess said. 'I couldn't wait for you.'

'That's fine. I'm glad you didn't wait.' Daniel was smiling as he lifted the green-striped teatowel. Everything was wonderful. He'd been talking to Lily. Life was good. 'Thanks for making all these sandwiches for me.'

'They're probably dried out and stale.' Jess eyed him sulkily. 'You were on the phone for hours.'

'Hardly hours, chicken.'

She jerked a thumb at the clock on the wall. 'Look at the time.'

'Well, Lily and I had a lot of news to catch up on.'

He bit into his first sandwich, hoping to avoid more questions.

Jess eyed him solemnly over a glass of milk. 'Is she the same Lily who left those stone people here?'

'Yes, that's right. She left them here for you.'

With a dramatic lift of one eyebrow, his sweet daughter made it patently clear that she wasn't particularly impressed by Lily's generosity.

Daniel set down his sandwich. 'Lily's also the friend who cleaned the house for me.' Surely Jess couldn't have found fault with that?

'And was she the person who threw the photo of Mummy and you in the rubbish bin?'

Shocked, Daniel stared at her, almost too stunned for words. How on earth had she found that photo?

'That's not Lily's fault. It was damaged beyond repair,' he said.

'No, it wasn't. Only the glass was broken.'

'Are—are you sure?'

'Yes.' Watching him, Jess tilted her chin defiantly. 'I took the picture out of the frame so I could keep it.'

'That was dangerous.' Daniel found it difficult to keep his voice calm. 'You could have cut yourself.'

'But I didn't.' She sent him a look of pure triumph.

Rather out of his depth, Daniel stared at his sandwich, then opened it and added a sprinkling of pepper.

'I'm sorry,' said Jess, suddenly contrite.

'Yes, well, I'm sure you'll be more careful next—'

'Not about the photo. I mean I'm sorry I forgot to put pepper on your tomatoes.'

It took a moment for him to take this in. 'No problem,' he said finally. 'I'm quite happy to pepper my own food.'

And then, hoping to restore the peace, he reached over and covered her hand with his. 'Actually, darling, I don't expect you to make my lunch. You've got better things to do on a Saturday.'

'But I want to do it.' There was an unmistakable urgency in the way she said this.

'You're certainly very good at making sandwiches. You're so grown-up now.'

She looked pleased. She smiled and sat tall, watching him as he bit into his bread and tomatoes, but scant minutes later she was solemn again. 'Did Lily make your sandwiches when she was here?'

Daniel swallowed. 'Yes. Sometimes.'

He remembered the curried-egg sandwiches they'd eaten on the riverbank after they'd made love, and his mouth twitched. He almost grinned.

'What's so funny?'

'I was just thinking of—of something.'

'Her.'

'Lily has a name, Jess. It's polite to use it.'

'You really like her, don't you?'

This was a direct challenge.

'Yes, I like Lily.'

'*Really* like her?'

'OK. Yes, I *really* like her.'

'Is she going to come here to live?'

Holy mackerel. He wasn't ready for this kind of interrogation. Not from Jess. Not from anyone.

'I'm not sure. Lily can't go anywhere at the moment. Her mother has to go into hospital, and she's going to be busy taking care of her.'

'She should stay with her mother,' the child said emphatically. 'We don't need her. I can look after you, Daddy. I can make sandwiches and cups of tea, and I can learn to cook dinners and—and clean things.'

She looked suddenly very vulnerable and very young. And frightened. Her eyes were huge, and her chin trembled.

One look at that quivering little mouth, and Daniel understood.

An instant later he was crouching at her side. 'Come here, baby.'

With a snuffling cry, Jess tumbled into his arms and buried her head into the curve of his chest. He cradled her close, and she was all long thin arms and long thin legs.

How quickly the years had flown. It seemed no time at all since she'd been a chubby ball of a baby, and then a laughing toddler, a cute-as-pie little girl in pigtails. Now she'd reached the awkward in-between age—on the very brink of growing up, but still so very young.

'Don't worry, duck,' he murmured, tucking her head beneath his chin. 'I know you've had a rough time, and I promise you nothing's going to change around here in a hurry.'

'I've only just got you back,' she whimpered.

'Yes, sweetheart. I know. I know. And I only just got you.'

'It's nice, just the two of us.'

'It is. It's wonderful, Jess.'

'It's only been us since I was four years old. I want it always to be the two of us,' she said. 'Just us and Smiley.'

CHAPTER NINE

'It's her,' Jess said, when the phone rang at breakfast about a week later. 'Lily.'

Daniel tried to keep his expression composed and neutral as he took the receiver. He and Lily had decided to make their phone calls late in the evening, after Jess was in bed, so he was surprised that she was ringing so early.

'I'm sorry, Daniel, I had to ring you,' Lily said. 'I'm so scared. Fern's just gone in. To the theatre.'

'So, they're operating now?'

'Yes.'

'She's going to be fine, Lily. She's in expert hands.'

'I know. But sometimes—I mean, in every operation there's always a chance, isn't there, that something might go wrong?'

It was on the tip of his tongue to tell her that this was a straightforward hip replacement, not open heart surgery, but he stopped himself just in time. After all, the fear in Lily's voice was genuine. 'Hey, this isn't like you. You're the girl who always looks on the bright side.'

'Am I?'

'Always.' Lily was steady and generous, sensuous and loving…

She let out a deep sigh. 'It's just that I bullied Fern into this. I chased the money and I lined up the doctor. It's a bad habit of mine—making people do what I think is best for them.'

'From what you've told me, I'm sure you're right about this.'

'If Fern had her way, she'd stay clear of hospitals.'

'But she's crippled and in pain, isn't she?'

'Yes,' Lily agreed. 'But, left to her own devices, if the pain got too much, she would be just as likely to have a party on the beach with lots of wine and then do the hippie thing.'

'What's that? Drifting out to sea on a raft of rose petals?'

'Something like that.'

'Lily, your mother will shower you with her gratitude when this is over, when she's fit and well again.'

'Oh, I hope so.'

Daniel leaned a casual shoulder against the wall and smiled. 'Take it from someone who has been bullied mercilessly by you—' He stopped in mid-sentence.

Through the kitchen window, he could see Jess and Smiley outside. Jess was directly in his line of sight, standing at the fence, and hurling something out across an empty paddock. At first he thought she was throwing something for Smiley to fetch, but then he realised it was a small stone.

'I bullied you into collecting Jess from Sydney,' Lily was saying. 'But that's worked out well, hasn't it?'

'Absolutely.'

Frowning, Daniel watched through the window as Jess hurled another stone, before turning back to look his way. Through the window, across the back yard, his daughter's eyes challenged him. Her jaw set stubbornly as, still watching him, she reached into the pocket of her school uniform and drew out another stone.

She was throwing away Lily's stone people. Daniel was sure of it.

The little minx. She was doing this to punish him. To punish Lily. Horrified, he watched as Jess drew her arm back, ready to throw the last stone.

'Stop it, Jess!' he cried through the open window, but he was too late. The third stone was already winging its way to the far end of the paddock.

'What's the matter?' asked Lily, on the other end of the line.

'Sorry. I was distracted for a moment.'

'I know I've called at a bad time. You've got to get Jess off to school.'

'Actually, yes,' he said, watching Jess and Smiley coming back together across the yard to the house. 'Can we speak later? I really hope everything goes well for your mother. I'll be thinking of you, Lily.'

'Thanks. I miss you so much, Daniel.'

Jess came into the kitchen.

'And I miss you, too,' he said, with deliberate tenderness.

Jess didn't look at him. She picked up the plates and cutlery they'd used for breakfast and carried them to the sink, suddenly a perfect and dutiful daughter, planning to do the washing up.

Behind her, Daniel hung up the phone. 'I can't believe you did that,' he said.

Jess turned with an expression of wide-eyed innocence. 'Are you talking to me?'

'You know I am.' He made no attempt to hide his anger. 'And you know what I'm talking about. Those were Lily's stone people you were hurling out there, weren't they?'

She looked only a little guilty.

'Why did you do it, Jess?'

She shrugged. 'I don't like them.'

'You don't like the stones? Or you don't like it when I talk to Lily?'

Jess refused to answer.

'Have you any idea how much those stones are worth?'

'No,' she said, looking puzzled.

'The man who painted them, Lily's father, was a very famous artist. Anything he painted—even those little stones—are worth a great deal of money.'

'I didn't know,' she said unhappily. 'You should have told me.'

Daniel could hardly admit that the monetary value of the stones had never been particularly important to him or Lily. He'd only mentioned it now because he was damn sure Jess wouldn't care about their sentimental value.

'I'm telling you now,' he said. 'And I'm telling you something else. You'll be spending your afternoons, after school, hunting in that paddock until you find those stones. All three of them.'

As Jess turned back to the washing up, Daniel had a sinking feeling that his life was veering off-track again. And just when everything had been going so well.

Jess had settled into school after only a few minor road-bumps. Her two best friends, Jane and Susie, were coming for a sleepover next weekend. He'd been particularly pleased that the girls' parents had agreed to it without any apparent qualms.

He'd begun to realise that his fears about people in the

district had been unfounded. He had plenty of support. People were pleased to see him back. Life was returning to normal.

Now Jess had to spoil it all by taking a dislike to Lily. To the idea of Lily. And he found himself wondering if it was too much to ask to have both Jess *and* Lily in his life.

'We're home!' Lily almost shouted down the phone when she rang ten days later. 'Fern's delirious with joy to be out of hospital and back under her own roof.'

'That's great news. And how are you feeling?'

'So happy I almost hugged the doctor when we said our goodbyes.'

She heard Daniel's deep, sexy chuckle.

'The poor man doesn't know what he missed,' he said.

'Oh, Daniel, you're the man I really need to hug. I wish I could see you. Telephones are wonderful inventions, but they have their limitations.'

'Yeah,' he agreed. 'No hugging potential at all.'

Lily sighed. She was finding this separation so much harder than she'd expected. She wished she was brave enough to ask Daniel how he really felt about being apart from her.

At Ironbark, there'd been so many unspoken reassurances from him—in the way his eyes lit up when he looked at her, in the way he touched her, the way he made love to her.

These days her mind threw up constant pictures of Ironbark, with its rolling paddocks and its sleepy, slow river, and the half-circle of ancient palm trees standing sentinel around the homestead. And she felt a deep longing—for Daniel and his home.

'Where are you now, Daniel? Which room in the house?'

'I'm in the study.'

'In that big brown leather chair with the high back?'

'Yes,' he said, sounding faintly amused. 'That's the one.'

'I can see you.' Smiling, she closed her eyes and imagined him there. 'You've taken your boots off and left them outside the back door, and you're just wearing socks. Navy blue ones. And you're leaning back in your chair with your long legs stretched out in front of you, crossed at the ankles.'

Daniel laughed.

'Am I right?'

'Spot-on,' he said. 'I can't believe I'm so predictable.'

'I can't believe I got to know you so well in under a week.' She spoke in a kind of hushed and awe-filled whisper as she realised how deeply she felt about this man.

'That was a very special time, Lily.'

Something about the way he said that scared her suddenly— a sense of things past, gone for ever and never to be retrieved.

'I won't be able to get away till Fern is strong again, but I was wondering if you and Jess could come here and visit us, now that we're back,' she said, needing to shake off that feeling of foreboding and rekindle the happiness and confidence that had filled her at the start of the conversation.

'Yeah,' said Daniel. 'That sounds great.'

'Sugar Bay's only about half a day's drive from your place. The weather's beautiful this time of year. Jess'll love the beach. It'll be fabulous. Let's set a date.'

'Maybe—'

Lily hurried on. 'And as soon as Fern's mobile again, I promise I'll come out to Ironbark to spend some time with you and Jess there.' Lily paused and waited for Daniel's answer. When it didn't come, she said, 'What do you think?'

Daniel sighed.

Her heart began an anxious thumping.

'I might— We might need a little more time, Lily.'

'I see,' she said slowly. But she didn't. She didn't see at all. She'd thought Daniel was as impatient to get back together as she was. 'So, you don't want to set a date?'

'I have to be honest with you. I don't think Jess is quite ready to deal with the idea of—us. As a couple.'

Lily sat very still, unable to speak. She looked dully about her at the bright mishmash of furnishings in Fern's sitting room and she thought, *This is it. It's happening all over again. As soon as I fall deeply, heart-and-soul in love with a man, it happens.*

Daniel was going to break it off. And she didn't know if she could bear it.

'Lily? Are you there?'

'Yes,' she said, praying that she wouldn't embarrass herself by bursting into tears.

'Jess has been rather difficult,' he said. 'There's been a lot for her to adjust to.'

'Yes, I understand.'

The worst of it was that she *did* understand. She could imagine herself in Jess's shoes at the age of eleven.

'I guess it's just like I warned you,' she said. 'Jess feels fiercely possessive about you now. I imagine she doesn't want to share you. Certainly not with a strange female.'

'That's it. You've pretty much hit the nail on the head. It helps that you understand.'

No, it doesn't, Lily thought, with a kind of wild desperation. *It doesn't help me at all.*

'And what about you, Daniel? How do you feel?'

She heard a soft sound on the other end of the line that might have been a groan or a sigh.

'It's a really delicate situation, Lily.'

She felt shaky, and she wanted to cry.

'I need to play it very carefully,' Daniel said. 'After all, I dragged Jess away from Sydney with the promise that her life back home would be just the way it used to be. As far as she's concerned, the way it used to be is just the two of us. That's how it's been since before she started school, and it's what she expected. It's what she wants. Right now, I don't know if she can handle the idea of anything more.'

There was something terribly final about the way he said that.

'That's—that's understandable.' Lily was grateful that she managed to sound together, even though she was terrified inside. She was gripped by a mad impulse to say, *I'll wait. I'll wait till Jess grows up and leaves home, if necessary.*

But she knew she couldn't begin to talk about a prolonged separation without breaking down. She'd been humiliated that way before. She'd tried to negotiate all sorts of pathetic bargains with Josh, when he'd first shown signs of wanting to leave her. She wasn't about to go down that path again.

'It's probably best if we call it quits now, isn't it?' she said, very hurriedly. 'Otherwise we might be trying to drag out something that's never going to work anyway. There's no point in prolonging the agony.'

'Lily—I—'

'I'm sorry, Daniel. I think I can hear Fern calling. I'd better go. Goodbye.' And she hung up.

I can't believe I let that happen.

Daniel sat in a horrified daze, staring at the telephone.

What have I done?

When he'd answered the phone and heard Lily's cheerful voice, he'd felt a leap inside him, like a shout of joy. It happened every time; whenever he thought of her he was instantly happy. Lily Halliday was the most exciting woman he'd ever met—lovely to look at, and so much fun to be with. Sensitive and loving. Divine in bed. She'd helped push away the darkness that had haunted him after prison.

Covering his face with his hands, he pressed his fingers against his eyes and stifled a cry of angry despair.

Lily was the woman he should have wooed and won.

He knew that with damning certainty. He'd never met anyone like her, and he never would again.

But how was a future with her possible? When she'd asked him to come to Sugar Bay he'd thought of Jess, and he'd known at once that the trip wouldn't work.

If he tried to leave Jess with a babysitter she would resent being farmed out, but if he took her to play gooseberry while he courted Lily she would be worse. She would pout and sulk. He would get angry. Lily would be upset. It would be a disaster all round.

And he couldn't, in all honesty, blame Jess.

The poor kid had already suffered enough at her parents' hands. A jailbird father and a runaway mother who had subsequently died were more than any child should have to deal with.

He couldn't dump a new set of hurdles in front of her. Not yet.

Damn, damn, damn. It was painful to accept, but he knew that Lily had probably been wise to end things between them.

Lily was young and beautiful. Wherever she went, there would be guys lining up to win her. Why should he expect her to hang around, waiting till he and Jess let go of their past and woke up to their future?

I can't believe I let him go.

Lily sat on the edge of the bed in her little room at the back of Fern's cottage, hugging her arms tightly over her stomach.

How could I do that?

How could she have broken up with Daniel? She was mad about the man. She was totally in love with him. Didn't he know that?

But his daughter loves him too, and she deserves him more.

There was the rub.

Lily had spent so many years feeling hurt about the way her own father had deserted her; she knew only too well how Jess must feel. She could imagine why Jess might want to put up barriers between Daniel and a new woman.

But the irony is that I was the one who sent him after you, Jess. I bullied and cajoled your daddy into reclaiming you. You want to cast me as some kind of wicked wannabe-stepmother. But I understand exactly how you feel.

It was so unfair.

If only she could fight for Daniel. Lily wanted to. Desperately. But she couldn't fight with his daughter. That was the one battle she would never begin, the single territory she dared not invade.

But, dear God, losing Daniel was too high a price; it was unbearable. Without him what was the point of anything?

A heart-rending wail of despair broke from her, and she fell backwards onto the bed, giving in to her tears. She felt as if her last chance of happiness was draining away.

CHAPTER TEN

IT WAS almost nightfall by the time Daniel and Jess walked back from the stockyards to the house. They took their time, enjoying the last of the day, while Smiley scampered around them, chasing after the stick Jess threw for her.

There was still plenty of warmth in the air as they walked through the last of the purple twilight. Cicadas buzzed in the trees, katydids peeped in the grass, and from the stockyards came the occasional bellow of a calf, missing its mother.

'I wish we could just order out for pizza tonight,' Jess said.

'Yeah, pizza would be handy. I must say, I'm not in the mood for cooking.' Daniel threw an arm around her skinny shoulders. 'You ever miss the big city?'

She smiled up at him and shook her head. 'Not really. Just some things, like take-away pizza and going to the movies.'

'Well, with a little planning we can get a frozen pizza from the supermarket for the weekend, and a movie from the video store.' As they reached the front steps, he suddenly remembered. 'Actually, I think Lily—' He broke off and cleared his throat. 'I think there's a pizza left in the freezer.'

Jess didn't respond.

But she didn't object, either, when Daniel found the frozen pizza and put it in the oven.

While it heated, and the aroma of tomatoes, mozzarella cheese and Italian herbs began to fill the kitchen, Daniel sat at the table and read the local paper, drinking a pre-dinner beer.

Jess filled Smiley's feeding bowl and poured orange juice into her favourite glass with stars painted on it, and then she sat at the other end of the table to begin her homework by searching through old magazines for pictures of tropical fruit.

It was a very cosy scene, Daniel supposed. Domestic bliss in a country farmhouse. Pity there was a vital someone missing from the scene.

Whoa, there. Mind-slip.

He mustn't allow himself to think about Lily. Whenever thoughts of her threatened, he used the old blanking-out routine. But every so often—about a thousand times a day—she'd slip though his defences. He'd think of her, and the deep, raw pain of losing her would catch him, like a lingering war-wound, bringing a rush of sweet, heartbreaking memories.

'Daddy, can I ask you something?'

Daniel looked up from the paper he wasn't really reading. 'Sure, Jess. Fire away.'

'What was it like in jail?'

He felt his stomach sink. 'Why do you want to know that?'

'Because you were there. For so long. And I hated not knowing how you were. When I was at Grandma's you sent me letters, and they were great, but you didn't say anything about what it was like, or what you were doing.'

'I'm sorry. I didn't think you'd want to know.'

'But I did. I still do.'

'Well…it wasn't much fun,' he said carefully.

'What was the worst thing?'

The worst thing. Had there been any one worst thing? Daniel didn't want to talk about it. He wanted to put it behind him, to protect Jess and keep it hidden.

She was watching him with wide, worried eyes, and he wondered what untold horror she was imagining. Perhaps he owed her the truth.

'The lack of privacy was the worst thing,' he said quietly. 'And I really found it hard to have someone else take total control over everything I did—what I wore, what I ate and how long I slept. I couldn't choose my company, or who I worked with.'

'Were the other men very awful?'

'Some of them. But not all. Things got better when I was moved to the prison farm.'

Jess hunted in her pencil case for a small pair of scissors, found them and began to cut out a bunch of bananas. 'Were you ever happy there?'

Daniel thought about lying, and changed his mind. 'No, Jess, I can't say I was. Maybe I should have found a way to be happy, but I didn't. I just wanted to get it over and done with.'

'What about now?' she asked quietly. 'Are you happy now you're home?'

Stunned by her question, he spluttered, 'Of course I'm happy.'

'Really happy, Daddy?'

Feeling cornered, he made an expansive gesture, taking in the glowing oven and Smiley wolfing down her dinner in the corner, the table scattered with Jess's school things and his newspaper.

'Look at me,' he said. 'I've got a fresh intake of calves out in the yard, the prettiest little daughter in Australia, a well-fed dog. A pizza in the oven. And you have to ask me if I'm happy?'

Jess pulled a face. 'You don't seem especially happy.'

He took a swift swig of his beer. 'Don't I?'

'Not the way you did when you first brought me home from Sydney. You were really, really happy then. All kind of bubbly and excited inside. But now you're just—I don't know. Not totally sad, but…' She eyed him with an incredibly grown-up kind of scrutiny. 'You look like you might be nursing a tormented heart.'

'Nursing a what?' Daniel stared at her in open-mouthed shock—shocked firstly that Jess should use such words, and secondly that she'd described so exactly how he felt.

He'd been trying so hard to keep his feelings under wraps. 'Where on earth have you heard about "tormented hearts"?'

She had the grace to blush, and she tapped her scissors against the cover of a magazine. 'I read it here. There's a story about a television actress whose boyfriend dumped her.'

The oven pinged, and Daniel seized the chance to jump up and look busy. He removed the pizza and set it on a round cane mat in the middle of the table.

'Get a load of this,' he declared, with forced enthusiasm. 'A perfectly melted and toasty pizza. Aren't you hungry, Jess? Come on. Where are the place mats and plates and napkins?'

He fetched a sharp knife, began to cut the pizza, and Jess hurried to collect the other necessary items from the dresser. But when they sat down to eat she only nibbled a little of her pizza slice, then set it back on her plate.

'What's the matter?' Daniel asked her. 'This is ham and pineapple. It's your favourite, isn't it?'

Instead of answering, she reached over to her school bag, which she'd left on a spare chair, and pulled a little drawstring bag from it. She set it, with a clunk, on the scrubbed pine table-top.

'I've found them all,' she said, and then she opened the strings. 'It took me ages.' Three painted stones tumbled out onto the table.

'Oh…' Daniel stared at them. 'That's…great.'

'You never checked to make sure I found them.'

'No, I guess I forgot.'

'They got a bit chipped.' She picked up the stone with the male face. Part of the nose was missing. 'This one's the worst. Sorry.'

'Jess, that's OK. I'm glad you found them, but you really should get on with your dinner. Pizza's not so hot when it's cold.'

He smiled at his joke, but Jess ignored it. She nibbled some crust. 'I'm not really hungry.'

'Of course you are. What's the matter? You're not sick, are you?'

She shook her head, but she continued to sit there, watching him, biting her lip and looking upset. Using her fingers, she picked a piece of pineapple from her pizza topping and popped it in her mouth. 'I'm worried,' she said at last.

'Why, sweetheart? What's the matter? Has something happened at school?'

Again, she shook her head, and this time she looked as if she might cry.

'Tell me what it is.' Daniel was getting more anxious every second, but he spoke in his most comforting, fatherly voice. 'Dads are pretty good at fixing things.'

'Well.' Jess heaved a huge sigh, as if what she had to say was very difficult to get out. 'Why don't you talk to Lily any more on the telephone?'

Whack!

Her question landed like a smart bomb—right on target, in the centre of his chest.

At first he couldn't think of a single answer, and then, lamely, he said, 'We've both been too busy.'

Jess rolled her eyes to the ceiling. 'I know that's not true.'

'Why do you mind anyway, Jess? You didn't want me to talk to Lily. You didn't like it when we talked.'

'But *you* liked it, Daddy,' Jess insisted. '*You* liked Lily. You shouldn't have stopped phoning her just because of me. Not if it makes you horribly sad.'

Daniel gaped at his daughter in dumbfounded dismay. What on earth had provoked her outburst? He'd been trying so hard to wipe Lily from his thoughts, trying not to be miserable—or at least not to let it show. For Jess's sake.

'When I was in Sydney, I tried to make everyone think I was happy,' Jess said. 'But I was only pretending. All the time, at school and at Grandma's, I was sad on the inside. Missing you.'

'Poor baby,' Daniel whispered, too choked to say more.

'I really, really don't want you to feel like that, Daddy.'

And then she burst into tears.

Lily pulled a cotton shift over her bikini and gathered up her beach things—sunglasses, hat, sunscreen, a paperback novel—and went through to the kitchen, where Fern was waiting for her.

'All set?' She was taking Fern to visit a friend at the other end of the bay that afternoon.

'Raring to go,' Fern said, and she rose from her chair with hardly any perceptible stiffness. She turned to collect her things from the kitchen counter, glanced up at her daughter, and frowned.

'Lily, dear, you look so tired.'

'Do I?'

'Yes.' Fern set her things down again, and peered more closely. 'Here am I, almost cured, and you, poor darling, are completely worn out.'

Lily suppressed an urge to sigh. 'I'm fine, Mum. Don't worry about me. Anyway, I'm going to spend a deliciously lazy afternoon on the beach.'

Fern's blue eyes were suddenly watchful. 'Will that help? Your problem isn't really physical exhaustion, is it?'

Ignoring the question, Lily snagged her car keys from the row of hooks on the wall. 'Come on. Let's go.'

'Wait, Lily. There's something I'd like to get clear.'

'What's that?'

'I know I'm a bit vague, and don't follow things through, but let me get this straight. When you came back from Gidgee Springs, I could tell that something wonderful had happened to you out there. Your eyes were alight with a special kind of happiness. And there was even talk of grandchildren and a "theoretical father". I know we were being playful about that, but then there were endless phone calls with a man who made you positively glow. And then nothing. What happened?'

There was a stretch of silence, during which Lily tried to answer, but couldn't.

Fern crossed the room, placed her hands very gently on her daughter's shoulders, and studied her face. 'I miss that wonderful light in your eyes. What happened, darling?'

'He's busy. He's a widower, and he's caring for his daughter and getting his cattle property back into working order.'

'Too busy for an occasional phone call?'

Lily blinked, and then was forced to close her eyes against the threat of tears. 'All right, Mum. You win. We broke up.'

We broke up. Three simple words. But so deeply distressing. They chilled the air in the cheery kitchen.

'My poor Lily,' Fern whispered, recognising the pain deeply buried in her daughter. 'I'm so sorry. What went wrong?'

'I'd rather not talk about it.'

'But I hate to see you so unhappy. You're still very much in love with this man, aren't you?'

Lily was gripping the car keys so tightly they cut into her. 'So much I can't bear it,' she whispered.

'Lily, can't you tell me how it happened? Why did you let him go?'

I was following in your footsteps, Lily thought, but she couldn't say that. 'I—I let him go because I knew it was for the best.' She winced—it sounded so lame.

'Best for whom?'

'For Daniel's daughter, Jess. And for him.'

'But what about you, Lily? Was it best for you?'

The question reverberated through her, and, horribly, there was only one answer. Losing Daniel was the worst, the very worst thing that had ever happened to her. Far worse than losing her father or Josh Bridges.

But there was no way Lily would admit it.

'That's enough,' she said sharply. 'I know you mean well, Mum, but I can't take any more of this interrogation.' She headed for the door. 'I'm taking you to Linda's. Grab your things and let's go.'

Sitting sphinx-still, with her arms locked around her knees, Lily stared out to sea. Her novel, a murder mystery, lay abandoned on her beach towel, while her mother's questions pushed and probed at her.

You're still very much in love with this man, aren't you? Why did you let him go? What about you, Lily? Was it best for you?

She thought again, as she had so many times in the past painful weeks, of that last, terrible telephone conversation with Daniel. Over and over she'd berated herself for being so impulsive, for suggesting that they shouldn't see each other, for hanging up on him. So many times she'd wanted to ring him back, to apologise, or at the very least to find out how he was. But she was too frightened.

I can't believe I'm such a wimp.

What was the matter with her? Where was the woman who'd driven off into the Outback to face up to Audrey Halliday? Where was the woman who'd bulldozed her way into Daniel Renton's life—in spite of his protests? Where was the feisty dame who'd charged into his home, bringing groceries and Smiley?

How could she have been so gutsy then, and so pathetic now?

Round and round the questions circled, and then suddenly, and with unexpected clarity, the answer came to her.

She'd faced up to Audrey, because Fern had needed the money. And she'd been bossy with Daniel because she'd known it was what he'd needed. And then she'd given up Daniel because it was what Jess needed.

Zap!!

The thought hit her like a lightning strike—*I can be brave when I'm doing it for someone else, but when it comes to what I want, I back down.*

She loved Daniel—loved him so much that every part of her ached with her need for him. Without him, she feared she might never be happy again.

And what was she doing about it?

Zilch.

She deserved better than that.

Yes!

Leaping up, she hauled her shift over her head, dropped it onto the towel and ran to the water. She gave a shout of exhilaration and dived in, slicing neatly beneath a cool, salty green wave.

Everything was perfectly clear in her head now. She would go back to Ironbark. She would face up to Daniel. She would win over his daughter. If necessary, she would fight—very nicely—for her right to be there with them. She was going to claim Daniel for herself—she would find a way. The thought was so exciting she was almost giddy. She swam quickly out to a little mound of rocks that marked a small inshore reef, and then she turned and swam back to the shallows again.

Jogging through the ankle-deep water, impatient to get to Fern and tell her this decision, she looked up.

There was a man walking down the beach, dressed in red and white Hawaiian-print board shorts. With Daniel on her mind, she thought for a crazy moment that the man *was* Daniel.

His beautifully wide shoulders and tapering lean waist were so much like Daniel's. And he had dark, thick hair like Daniel's, and he walked like—

Oh, goodness.

Lily felt as if she'd fallen into the vast blue void of a bottomless ocean.

It *was* Daniel.

It was Daniel, with a slender, laughing, dark-haired girl skipping beside him. She was wearing a lime-green two-piece swimsuit, and she was at that in-between age—all skinny arms and legs—but there was an unmistakable grace about the way she moved. She had to be Jess.

Father and daughter were chatting and laughing as they set their towels and a striped beach-bag down on the sand. And then, squinting slightly against the glare, Daniel looked Lily's way. Her heart threatened to burst through her chest, and the bravado she'd felt thirty seconds ago vanished.

What was he doing here?

He shaded his eyes and took another look at her, and she wondered if he would recognise her. With her hair wet and stringy, dressed in a bright floral bikini, she probably looked like a dozen other girls at the beach.

But he was grinning and coming across the sand, calling hello.

Lily could see the crinkling of skin around his eyes as he smiled, the sky-blue of his irises. She began to shake. Why was he here? In her entire life, she had never felt so nervous.

He looked nervous, too, in spite of the smile. He stopped some feet away. No kiss hello.

She said, somewhat breathlessly, 'This is a surprise.'

'I know. I'm sorry I didn't warn you we were coming. It was a spur-of-the-moment decision.'

Why? She couldn't bring herself to ask that, so she said, 'And you've brought Jess. On a school day?'

He looked back over his shoulder to Jess, who was standing by their things, watching them with hugely curious eyes. 'Hey, Jess,' he called. 'Come and meet Lily.' To Lily, he said, 'It doesn't hurt for her to miss a day of school once in a blue moon.'

His eyes moved restlessly over her, taking in details—her hair, wet and clinging, her floral bikini, and her suntan, deeper now after more than a month at the bay.

She thought of the last time she and Daniel had been together. The final blissful night of passion. And, irrationally, she felt embarrassed and self-conscious to be wearing so little now. She wished she'd had time to cover up.

'It's so good to see you,' he said.

'You, too.'

Jess arrived, and there were introductions. The girl smiled at Lily shyly. They talked for a bit about swimming, and the pretty coral fish on the little reef out near the rocks.

But all the time they chatted Lily wondered why they had come. What did this mean? 'When did you arrive?' she asked.

'Not long ago,' Daniel told her. 'We went to your house first, but there was no one home, so we decided to drive along the bay, have a swim, and check again later.'

'So, you've come to see me?' Her heart raced.

'Of course.' Daniel's eyes were intense as he looked at her, but he was still smiling. 'Why else would we be here?'

Lily, in a kind of dreamlike haze, said, 'Mum's with a

friend. I'm about to collect her. But we'll be back at the house soon. You're very welcome.'

'We'll be there, just as soon as Jess has had a swim and we've cleaned up. We're booked into the motel out on the point.'

'Right.' It was ridiculous to still be so nervous. 'See you soon then. You must stay for dinner. Have a nice swim, Jess. Bye, Daniel.'

Fern accepted the news of Daniel's arrival without making a fuss. She didn't ply Lily with questions on the way back to the cottage. She seemed quite content with her own conclusions.

When they found an enormous bouquet of white lilies and a basket of maidenhair fern set in a shady corner of the front porch, she wasn't at all surprised.

Lily stared at them. Lilies and ferns. 'Daniel must have left these.'

'Of course he did, darling. Aren't they gorgeous? How thoughtful.' Fern's eyes were sparkling. She seemed very excited, as if she could hardly contain herself.

Lily felt compelled to issue a warning. 'Mum, I have no idea what this visit is about.'

'Yes, you do, Lily. Trust me. These lovely gifts are a very good omen.'

They put the basket of ferns on the little table under the kitchen window, and the gorgeous white lilies in an enormous round glass jug on the coffee table in the lounge. The lilies' beautiful perfume made the little cottage smell heavenly.

'I've invited Daniel and Jess to stay for dinner,' Lily said, and she opened the door of the fridge and peered in. 'I could do that chicken and almond dish.'

'I don't think that will be necessary. Daniel will take you out to dinner, and Jess and I will have something simple here. Macaroni cheese.'

'You can't count on that at all.'

Fern flicked a knowing glance through the kitchen doorway to the vase of lilies, and then back to her daughter.

'That man is courting you, Lily.'

'But you don't understand the full picture, Mum. It's complicated. Jess doesn't want us to get together. That's why we broke up. That's why—' She looked down and fiddled with a button on her pocket. 'That's why I have no idea what's going on. I don't understand why Daniel's turned up like this. The suspense is killing me.'

'Oh, darling.' Fern crossed the room and gave her a hug. 'Be brave, Lily. Hang in there. It's going to be all right.'

'How can you possibly know that?'

'Motherly intuition.'

'Sorry. That's not scientifically reliable.'

'You've been a perfect angel looking after me, Lily. This is a thank-you gift from the universe.' Fern winked. 'Besides, I read your tea leaves at breakfast this morning.'

'Oh, Mum.' Lily gave her arm a playful punch, and pulled away. 'I think I'll take a bath.'

'Good idea.'

'Hold it, Dad,' Jess called as they were about to leave the motel. 'Turn around.'

'Jess, we're late. I don't have time—'

'Just turn around. I want to make sure you look nice.'

Daniel, so nervous he felt sick, turned. 'I didn't want to look too dressed-up,' he said.

Jess narrowed her eyes as she studied his open-necked white shirt with the long sleeves rolled back, his blue jeans, his neatly shaved jaw and his damp hair, carefully combed. She gave him the thumbs-up signal. 'Totally hot, Dad. Lily will love you.'

'Totally hot? Is that better than totally cool?'

She grinned. 'Don't worry. You look hot *and* cool.'

'You've lost me.' With a rueful smile, and a hand on Jess's shoulder, he shepherded her out through the door. 'Come on. Let's go.'

Fern appeared at Lily's bedroom door. 'A utility truck has just pulled up outside,' she said.

From the street came the slam of a car door. And then another. Lily's heart jumped each time. She turned to the mirror. She was wearing a simple dress in swirling aqua-blue, with thin shoulder straps and a softly flaring skirt. Daniel had never seen her in a dress. She'd added gold earrings and low-heeled sandals, and she'd left her legs bare.

'Do I look as if I'm trying too hard?'

'You look perfect.'

They shared a smile.

'Shall I answer the door or will you?' Fern asked.

'I'd better go.'

On the doorstep, Jess said, 'Dad, we forgot the chocolates and wine. They're still in the glovebox.'

'Damn.' Daniel turned, about to head back to the car, but there was a sound of footsteps coming to the door.

'I'll go,' said Jess. 'Give me the car keys.'

She scampered back down the path just as the door opened.

Daniel knew Lily would look lovely, but even so the sight of her stole his breath.

'Hello again,' he said, in a voice barely above a whisper.

'Hi.'

Her eyes shone and she smiled at him. Leaning forward, he dropped a light kiss on her flushed cheek. Her skin felt wonderfully soft, and she smelled divine.

'I thought Jess was with you.' Lily looked suddenly worried.

'She's just getting something from the car.'

'We forgot these,' Jess called, madly waving a box of ginger chocolates and a bottle of red wine as she ran back up the path. She presented them to Lily. 'They're really from Dad, of course.'

'Oh, lovely. Thank you.' Lily smiled at her. 'And it's lovely to see you here, Jess.'

Jess met her gaze and smiled shyly. 'Thank you.'

Lily stepped back into the hall. 'Please, both of you, come on in.'

'This is a lovely house,' Jess said.

At first Lily thought the child was simply being polite—a little girl instructed to be on her best behaviour. But then she saw Jess's face, and the obvious delight with which she was looking about her.

The timber beach cottage was simple, shabby and old, and yet, thanks to Fern's artistic talent—the talent that had interested Marcus so many years ago—her home had undeniable charm. The walls, ceilings, windowsills and frames were all painted in a surprising but very appealing array of bright colours. Plants abounded in all manner of hand-painted pots. A lovely leadlight feature caught the last of the afternoon sun. Suspended in an open window, a mobile made from driftwood, shells and sea glass spun in the breeze. A collection of handmade candles nestled on another windowsill.

'These are so pretty,' Jess said, looking at the gorgeous-coloured candles decorated with pressed flowers.

'I could show you how to make a candle like that,' Fern told her.

'Could you?'

'Lily knows how to make them, too.'

'Oh, wow.'

Jess sent Lily another shy smile. And then she looked at Daniel. 'Go on, Daddy. I'm OK. Off you go.'

There was an awkward moment, where Daniel tried to shush Jess and Lily wasn't quite sure what was going on.

Fern took command.

'Your daughter's right, Daniel. You and Lily should take a walk. Jess and I want to get acquainted—don't we, Jess?'

'Sure,' the girl agreed, without a beat of hesitation.

Lily swallowed a surprised gasp. Since when had her mother become so bossy—and Jess so co-operative?

She looked at Daniel. He seemed so tall and big in Fern's tiny house. So handsome. His eyes burned with an intense light that made her heart flutter. She didn't think a heart could do such a thing, but, yes, it actually fluttered. With apprehension. With hope.

Daniel addressed Fern. 'I wouldn't normally rush off. There's a great deal I'd like to tell you about your wonderful daughter.'

Fern blinked, and reached in her pocket for a handkerchief.

'That would be lovely, Daniel, but I might blubber and get sentimental.'

'Mum!'

Fern winked at them. 'Off you two go. I'm going to show Jess my collection of beads.'

Daniel turned to Lily. 'Want to take a walk?'

What was she to say, but, 'I'd like that. Thank you.'

He took her hand, and her fingers burned at his touch. They left the house via the door that led to the beach, and at the gate, where the garden ended and the beach began, they removed their footwear. Daniel rolled up his jeans.

And then they set off across the still-warm sand. A breeze blew in from the sea, bringing the smell of salt and the tang of coral, lifting strands of Lily's newly washed hair and Daniel's shirt collar.

She said, 'I might never recover from the shock of seeing you turn up here, out of the blue.'

'I should apologise,' said Daniel. 'But I balked at the thought of another phone call. I didn't want to mess things up like last time. I needed to see you.'

'It's hard to get things right over the phone.'

'Yes.' His grip on her hand tightened. 'Lily, I don't know what your plans are now that Fern is on the mend, but I was wondering if...'

He stopped, looked stricken, and ran a hand through his wind-blown hair. 'I'm doing this badly. I haven't told you how much I've missed you, how amazing it is to see you again.' He took both her hands in his. 'How I feel about you, Lily.'

She looked up and saw the truth of it in his eyes, and her heart was so full she couldn't speak.

'I don't know how I've survived these past few weeks,' Daniel said. 'It's been worse than anything I felt in jail.'

She recognised the dark pain that lay behind his words. 'I've been the same, Daniel. I've been so miserable.'

'Would you consider coming back?'

'To live with you?'

His throat worked. 'Yes.'

Across the kitchen table, Jess said to Fern, 'Do you think my dad and Lily are in love?'

'Yes, my dear, I do.'

Jess, under Fern's supervision, was threading beads to make an anklet. Fern picked out a marvellous purple bead with tiny chips of silver mirror. 'Would you like this one?'

'Oh, wow! Yes, please.'

'Would you mind if Lily and your father decided that they're very much in love and want to stay together?'

Jess shook her head. 'Not now. Not now I understand.'

Fern smiled at her. 'And what is it that you understand?'

'That Dad couldn't help falling for Lily. She's right for him.' Jess set the threaded beads down carefully, so she could concentrate on what she was saying. 'I saw the way Dad and Lily looked at each other, and something just seemed to click inside me. It felt right. I don't know if I can explain it any better than that.' She frowned. 'Maybe it's like a joke.'

'A joke?'

'You know how it is with a joke. People either get it or they don't. I "got it" that they're right for each other.'

Fern smiled and reached out to squeeze Jess's hand. 'I "got it", too.'

* * *

'I thought Jess objected to us,' Lily said, as they wandered along the almost deserted beach while the daylight faded around them.

'I've sorted things out with her.'

'How? Are you sure? It seems too good to be true.'

Daniel's mouth tilted into a wry curve. 'Jess could see for herself that I was a hopeless case without you. And then I told her exactly what you mean to me.' He tightened his arm about her shoulders. 'I told her how much I love you, Lily. I told her how you rescued me.'

'Rescued you?'

'Of course. If you hadn't run out of petrol and stumbled onto Ironbark I'd still be a depressed and broken man.' He smiled, but his eyes glittered with a sheen that rocked her heart. 'I might never have recovered from the shame and the horror of prison. Without you, I'd never have been strong enough to go to Sydney to reclaim Jess. I owe everything to you.'

'Oh, Daniel.' She lifted her hand and fingered a wing of dark hair blown onto his forehead, traced the dear, familiar ruggedness of his cheek with her fingertips. It was so, so good to touch him at last. 'How did Jess react?'

'She couldn't get me here fast enough.'

On a heady wave of relief and sheer joy, Lily let out a cheer, and she spun in a quick, ecstatic pirouette.

Daniel caught her with two hands at her waist. 'I love you, Lily.'

'I know,' she cried, laughing and crying as she hugged him hard. 'I know, I know, I know. And I love you, too!'

He kissed her. He took a deliciously long time about it, and Lily doubted there had ever been a kiss quite so perfect.

Later, he said, 'I would have been here yesterday if I hadn't bought a new mob of calves. To be honest, I shouldn't really be here now. I should be checking that they've settled in OK.'

A small wave lapped at Lily's ankles. 'The joys of a cattleman's life.'

He drew a sharp breath. 'Lily, is there any chance that you would consider sharing that life with me?'

Smiling, she shook her head at him. 'Can't you guess, Daniel Renton? From the very first day I walked onto Ironbark I've been fantasising about spending my life with you. You were a marked man.'

'You mean I didn't stand a chance?'

'Not one.'

Daniel smiled. 'That was the luckiest day of my life.'

'And mine.'

And, for that, he pulled her into his arms and kissed her again.

Afterwards, he asked, 'Are we expected back at the house for dinner?'

She laughed. 'Actually, no. You're supposed to be taking me out for a romantic dinner.'

'Are you sure? Will Fern mind?'

'No, it's written in the tea leaves that Fern and Jess will have macaroni cheese, while you wine me and dine me at the lovely new restaurant attached to your motel.'

He looked amused. 'I didn't know you read tea leaves.'

'I don't. Fern does. She's an expert.'

Daniel grinned. 'Then we mustn't let the expert down.'

EPILOGUE

LILY watched through the weathered timber stock rails as Daniel deftly secured a young steer and began the process of vaccinating and ear-tagging. He worked quickly and smoothly in a carefully timed succession of movements, ensuring that the animal wasn't stressed for any longer than was strictly necessary.

He must have felt her gaze on him, and he looked up, glancing quickly her way. In that fleeting instant, in the midst of his busy work, his bright blue eyes met hers, and he winked and grinned at her.

That was all it took.

Lily melted.

His clothes were covered with dust, he was hot and tired, but he was strong and lean and gorgeous, and he was Daniel. He was her man—her lover. Her husband.

'Next!' he called.

Oh, dear, she'd been caught daydreaming. It was her turn to send the last calf down the race to him.

Left till last, the young steer had become anxious and frisky, and Lily had trouble rounding it up, but eventually it was on its way down the timber-fenced race. Minutes later, the day's work was completed. A new herd was in the holding yard, chomping quietly on the choicest hay, the ordeal of their initiation on Ironbark already forgotten.

Lily and Daniel, with Smiley in tow, began to walk back to the house. Daniel linked his hand with Lily's. She felt the familiar tough skin on his palm, and couldn't hold back a moment longer.

'I have some news,' she said.

Smiling indulgently, he squeezed her hand. 'What is it?'

'When I was in Gidgee Springs yesterday, I went to see Dr Barnes.'

Daniel frowned, his eyes suddenly serious, full of unspoken questions.

'It's good news,' she hastened to assure him.

He watched her cautiously. 'So, tell me.'

'I'm pregnant.'

He stopped dead in his tracks and stared at her. He frowned again, and shook his head. A tiny smile appeared, briefly lighting his eyes and lifting a corner of his mouth. And then it vanished, and his mouth twisted downwards and he looked worried. Upset.

'You don't mind, do you?' Lily whispered, suddenly frightened by his reaction.

'Did you say Dr Barnes told you this yesterday?'

'Yes.'

'Why didn't you tell me then?'

Lily dropped her gaze to her dusty riding boots. 'I thought you might not let me help in the stockyards today if you knew.'

He cursed softly. 'Damn right, I wouldn't!' Groaning, he put his arms around her and held her close.

'Nothing happened, Daniel. I'm fine.'

'That's not the point.'

'I'm sorry,' she said. 'I didn't think you'd be upset. You know I love helping you with the cattle.' Her chin lifted stubbornly. 'I'm sure I'm not the first pregnant cattleman's wife who's ever done a little yard work.'

Daniel jerked his gaze away from her and stared out across the paddocks, his face set and hard.

And Lily was struck by a terrible thought. 'Daniel, are you angry because I didn't tell you I'm pregnant? Or are you upset because you don't want a baby?' She couldn't keep a note of fear from her voice.

His head whipped around. For heart-stopping seconds his eyes were fierce as he searched her face. And then, at last, his expression softened. 'Oh, Lily, darling girl, of course I want our baby.'

And as he pulled her closer, hugged her, it didn't matter that they were hot and dusty and sweaty.

'We're going to have a baby,' he said, sounding suddenly excited, as if the truth of her words was only now hitting home.

'Yes, darling. That's what I said.'

'You're pregnant. I'm going to be a father again.' His face split into a grin, and he let out a shriek of delight.

'So, you're pleased?' she asked.

'Pleased? At the thought of our baby? Are you kidding, Lily? I'm ecstatic. I'm rapt. I'm over the moon!' He caressed the side of her head with his jaw. 'But you've brought out my protective instincts, too. No more yard work.'

'All right.' It was, after all, rather sweet of him to want to protect her. 'I can't wait to tell Jess when she comes back from Susan's.'

Daniel grinned. 'She'll be over the moon too.'

Suddenly he released her, and let out a whooping great shout of triumph. Before Lily knew what was happening, he turned and raced to the middle of the paddock. There, he cupped his hands to his mouth, tipped his head back and let out a yell.

'*Lu-cy! Jenn-i-fer! Agapanthus!*'

'What on earth are you doing?' Lily shouted.

Daniel grinned back at her. 'I'm giving our baby's name a test-yell.' Again he tipped back his head. 'Gwen-do-line!'

'Hey, wait a minute.' Lily charged across the paddock to join him. 'What's with all the girls' names? I want our baby to be a boy.'

'Do you?' Daniel's eyes danced with happiness. His mouth twitched with amused delight.

'Yes!' she cried. And now it was her turn to yell. '*Pe-ter! An-drew! Nebuchadnezzar!*'

Daniel watched her with a possessive, teasing smile. 'I guess I have no objection to a son,' he said. And, tipping his head back, he shouted, 'Ben-ja-min!'

'That's better.' Lily grinned at him. 'And I suppose a baby girl would be fine too.' She lifted her face towards the setting sun and yelled, 'Soph-ie!'

And then, absurdly happy, they fell into each other's arms.

In the middle of the big empty paddock they stood, laughing and hugging and sharing ecstatic kisses, until at last the lengthening shadows reached them and the sun dipped low behind the distant hills. Then they called to Smiley to stop sniffing for bandicoots, and, together with her, they headed for home.

* * * * *

Next month in
THE NANNY AND THE SHEIKH (#3928),
Barbara McMahon sweeps you away
to the exotic kingdom of Qu'Arim
in the next installment of
THE BRIDES OF BELLA LUCIA.

Years ago Sheikh Surim Al-Thani was called back to his kingdom Qu'Arim following the sudden death of his father. He determined to be a mature and responsible ruler, dedicated to his people. But when his cousin's three children were tragically orphaned, they came to the palace to be raised by the sheikh. Surim had no idea how to deal with the children or their grief. But now a chance encounter with professional nanny Melissa Fox offers a temporary solution… But can she heal the heart of the sheikh?

Sunday morning, Max and Melissa caught an early flight to Rome where they changed for a plane to Qu'Arim. It was late afternoon when they landed. Immediately after exiting the plane, Melissa raised her face to the sun. Its warmth felt fabulous! The air was perfumed with the sweet scent of plumeria mixed with that of airplane fuel. The soft breeze that wafted across her skin felt as silky as down. Soon they'd be away from the airport and she could really enjoy scents that vied for identification.

"I already love it here," she said as they walked across the tarmac.

"Did you say something?" Max asked, a bit distracted. He was in full business mode, having worked on the plane and now carrying his briefcase almost as if it were a part of him. Melissa wasn't surprised. The man loved his work. He ate, slept and breathed it as far as she could tell. Though he wasn't a hermit. He did his fair share of dating, according to her mother.

"It's nice here," she said, trying to match his businesslike attitude. Inside, however, she felt sheer excitement. She hoped she had some free time to explore while she was here. And maybe spend an afternoon at the beach. The Persian Gulf had been a heavenly blue when they had circled preparing to land.

They were met inside the terminal by a tall man with dark hair and almost black eyes. He smiled at Max when he spotted him and Melissa felt her heart skip a beat. She'd thought Max handsome, but this guy was something else! His charcoal-gray suit and red power tie were very western. She glanced around; most of the men wore suits, few wore the more traditional Arab robes.

In fact, she could have been in any airport in Europe. For a moment she was disappointed. She wanted to see more the exotic aspects of this country, not find it was just like any other capital she'd seen.

Melissa spotted two men standing nearby, scanning the crowd. The local equivalent of guards, she guessed from the way they behaved.

Max turned and made the introductions. Sheikh Surim Al-Thani inclined his head slightly, reaching for Melissa's hand and bringing it to his lips. The warmth of his lips startled her, but it was the compelling gaze in those dark eyes that mesmerized. She felt her heart race, heat flooded through her and she wondered if he came with a warning label—dangerous to a woman's equilibrium.

"Welcome to Qu'Arim," he said formally, his voice deep and smooth with the faintest hint of accent. "I hope your stay will be enjoyable. Please let me know if there is anything I can provide for you while you are here."

"Thank you," Melissa mumbled, feeling halfway infatuated by the sheer animal magnetism she sensed in the man. She could listen to him all day. His hand was warm and firm, almost seeming to caress before he released hers. She felt a fluttering of awareness at his intensity when he looked at her. Giving herself a mental shake, she tried to think of the mundane reason for her visit. She was definitely not here to get a crush on Max's friend.

She glanced back and forth between the two men as they spoke. Both carried an air of assurance and confidence that was as appealing as their looks. But it was Surim who captured her attention. Before she could think about it further, their host gestured toward the entrance.

Their small group began to move toward the front of the airport. She gladly let Max and Surim talk together while she looked eagerly around, taking in the crowds of travelers in the various dress. There was a mixture of languages, some she recognized as European. She wondered how hard it would be to learn some Arabic while she was here.

Melissa and Max were ushered into a luxurious stretch limousine while one of the men attending the sheikh went to fetch their luggage. Melissa settled back in her seat and gazed at the landscape, trying to ignore the growing sense of awareness she felt around the sheikh. He joined them after speaking to his men and Melissa was hard pressed not to stare. Resolutely she gazed out the window.

Flowers and soaring palms lined the avenue, softening the austere lines of the airport terminal.

As the sheikh continued his discussion with Max as the limo pulled away from the airport she occasionally glanced in his direction, intrigued as never before. Surim Al-Thani was slightly shorter than Max, but at six feet still towered over her own five feet three inches. His dark hair gleamed. She wondered if it was as thick and silky as it looked.

When he met her gaze she felt flustered. She had been rude. Yet when his eyes caught hers for an instant she continued boldly staring—this time directly into his dark gaze. Growing uncomfortably warm, Melissa finally broke contact and again looked out the side window. Her heart skipped a beat, then pounded gently in her chest.

Let *Margaret Way* enchant you with
these tales from the outback.

Introducing

Outback Marriages

these bush bachelors are looking for a bride!

Outback Man Seeks Wife

BY MARGARET WAY

On sale January 2007

Cattle Rancher,
Convenient Wife

BY MARGARET WAY

On sale March 2007

nocturne™

**WAS HE HER SAVIOR
OR HER NIGHTMARE?**

HAUNTED

LISA CHILDS

Years ago, Ariel and her sisters were separated for
their own protection. Now the man who vowed
revenge on her family has resumed the hunt, and
Ariel must warn her sisters before it's too late.
The closer she comes to finding them, the more
secretive her fiancé becomes. Can she trust the man
she plans to spend eternity with? Or has he been
waiting for the perfect moment to destroy her?

On sale December 2006.

REQUEST YOUR FREE BOOKS!
2 FREE NOVELS PLUS 2
FREE GIFTS!

H A R L E Q U I N   R O M A N C E®

From the Heart, For the Heart

YES! Please send me 2 FREE Harlequin Romance® novels and my 2 FREE gifts. After receiving them, if I don't wish to receive any more books, I can return the shipping statement marked "cancel." If I don't cancel, I will receive 4 brand-new novels every month and be billed just $3.57 per book in the U.S., or $4.05 per book in Canada, plus 25¢ shipping and handling per book and applicable taxes, if any*. That's a savings of over 15% off the cover price! I understand that accepting the 2 free books and gifts places me under no obligation to buy anything. I can always return a shipment and cancel at any time. Even if I never buy another book from Harlequin, the two free books and gifts are mine to keep forever.

114 HDN EEV7   314 HDN EEWK

Name	(PLEASE PRINT)	
Address		Apt.
City	State/Prov.	Zip/Postal Code

Signature (if under 18, a parent or guardian must sign)

Mail to Harlequin Reader Service®:

IN U.S.A.	IN CANADA
P.O. Box 1867	P.O. Box 609
Buffalo, NY	Fort Erie, Ontario
14240-1867	L2A 5X3

Not valid to current Harlequin Romance subscribers.

Want to try two free books from another line?
Call 1-800-873-8635 or visit www.morefreebooks.com.

* Terms and prices subject to change without notice. NY residents add applicable sales tax. Canadian residents will be charged applicable provincial taxes and GST. This offer is limited to one order per household. All orders subject to approval. Credit or debit balances in a customer's account(s) may be offset by any other outstanding balance owed by or to the customer. Please allow 4 to 6 weeks for delivery.

HR06

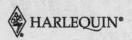

HARLEQUIN®

HARLEQUIN ROMANCE®

Coming Next Month

#3927 OUTBACK MAN SEEKS WIFE Margaret Way
Outback Marriages

Returning to his dilapidated ranch, Clay Cunningham intends to settle down and find himself a wife. Local-girl Caroline McNevin is as fragile and innocent as Clay is proud and rugged. Something in her vulnerability touches Clay, but first Caroline needs to confront her past.

#3928 THE NANNY AND THE SHEIKH Barbara McMahon
The Brides of Bella Lucia

Melissa Fox's trip to the kingdom of Qu'Arim is a perk of her job at Bella Lucia. When she expertly calms Sheikh Surim Al-Thani's three little children, he is determined she will stay on as his nanny. Soon she finds herself falling for a man she could only ever dream of marrying.

#3929 THE BUSINESSMAN'S BRIDE Jackie Braun

Art photographer Anne Lundy was proud of her independence. But when she needed help from straitlaced family-friend Richard Danton, Anne found herself unexpectedly attracted to him—and eager to find out what would happen if he lost control.

#3930 MEANT-TO-BE MOTHER Ally Blake

Single-father James Dillon has dedicated his life to his young son. Yet when a beautiful stranger appears on his doorstep, he can't ignore the magnetism between them. Siena Capuletti didn't mean to fall in love; can she overcome the mistakes of the past for the sake of James and his adorable son?